# OVER AND OUT

**By G B Ralph**

# OVER AND OUT
## Rise and Shine – Book Three

## G B RALPH

ISBN 978-0-473-59075-8 (Paperback POD)
ISBN 978-0-473-59076-5 (Epub)
ISBN 978-0-473-59077-2 (Kindle)

A catalogue record for this book is available from the National Library of New Zealand.

G B Ralph
www.gbralph.com

For my family and friends,
for taking the time to support these books
when there's already so much else going on.

# Chapter 1
# Who's to say this won't be the same?

## ARTHUR

'Bingo!'

Desmond sprung up, sending his collapsible chair flying backwards. The abrupt manoeuvre set off a chorus of alarm from the dabbers behind him. He ignored the protests in his eager shuffle to the front of the makeshift bingo hall which belied his advanced years.

'I knew it – could feel it in these old bones, you see. Here it is, Mr Wonka,' he said, waving the card in the air before slamming it down on my table, 'the golden ticket.'

'And how sure are we today?' I said, well aware of Desmond's tendency to stir up trouble when he'd decided a game had dragged on too long. On occasions I caught him fabricating a win, he would brush it off, blaming the error on senility. Though, we all knew he was still in complete control of his full set of marbles. He didn't help his case when he coupled these announcements with a mischievous wink.

'I trust you'll find everything's in order,' the old man said with a look of mock indignation. Then when I didn't respond right away he added, 'You doubt my sincerity, young man?'

'I would never,' I said, smiling at Desmond's theatrics.

'And while you're busy validating my honour – unimpeachable, I assure you – I thought I may take this opportunity to remind my fellow geriatrics of tomorrow's outing?'

I waved him on as I checked his numbers. Though nominally in charge of bingo night – calling the numbers, checking tickets, distributing prizes – I still saw myself as a guest. Sunset Villas was their home and my weekly appearances didn't give me the clout to refuse a resident, especially one such as Desmond – he'd do as he pleased. And, considering my attendance was expected for tomorrow's outing, I was intrigued to see what was planned. I hadn't had the heart to turn down the invite. Besides, Desmond assured everyone it would be an entertaining day out, and I had plenty of leave owing at work.

'All right, quiet down you old coots,' Desmond said to the seated bingo players. 'I know you're all *dying* to know what tomorrow's outing will entail. Now, I won the right to organise this outing and I've put a fair bit of planning into it, so don't you go knocking boots with old Mr Reaper in your dreams tonight – you'll be no good to us on the slab.'

This comment was met with huffs of disapproval and superstitious hand movements from around his audience.

'Besides,' Desmond continued, 'it might be rather

dispiriting for those of us with one foot still soundly out of the grave. So, if you're feeling anxious, perhaps you can borrow a couple of Maud's heavy-duty pills to get you through the heightened anticipation.'

I glanced up from checking Desmond's ticket to see Maud looking her usual serene self, hands clasped on the designer handbag resting on her knees and nodding along vacantly to Desmond's spiel. She didn't play bingo, but enjoyed being amongst the action – that's what I presumed anyway, seeing as she was here week after week.

'Come now, Dez.' That was Nora, our resident heckler. 'Just tell us, you old tease.' She was as bad as Desmond when it came to stirring, and a shameless flirt to boot. I'd have to supervise her, determined as the old girl was to have her way with me. She might try her luck tomorrow, fuelled by the day's adventures and unfamiliar surroundings.

'Calm yourself, Nora – you'll find out on the coach. Which – everyone listening? – will leave from out the front at nine on the dot. So, fire up those walking frames nice and early because latecomers will be left—'

'Will Arthur be joining us?' Nora said, cutting across Desmond.

'Yes, I believe he will,' he said, turning to me for confirmation.

I paused, then nodded – if I wasn't committed before, I was now. Nora smiled in return. She was plotting something and wasn't concerned if I knew.

'And what about this secret lover, hmm?' Nora wasn't even pretending to direct her query to Desmond anymore. 'Will we be introduced tomorrow, too? Or do you plan to keep this mystery beauty squirrelled away forever?'

9

'I – uh – no,' I said. 'It's just, you know, much too short notice. University and work commitments – another shift at the driving range – all that. And we hardly know each other, not ready to go introducing h—'

'What's it been, my boy – a fortnight?' Gerry said, cutting off my rambling in his warm, deep voice. I was grateful for the interruption.

'Uh, yeah.' Two weeks... was that all? It felt like a lot longer since we'd first run into each other – literally.

'There you have it, Nora. The kids are still getting acquainted with each other. When I was a young buck courting my Ava, I certainly wasn't willing to share her with my grandmother's friends on a geriatric day trip. We had other, more *youthful* ideas about how we wanted to spend our time together.' A few titters from the listening players met this remark. 'So, Nora, you let the boy take his time. We'll get to meet young Arthur's special someone soon enough.' He winked at me, and I smiled my cautious gratitude in return.

Gerry always had my back, though I remember being terrified of him as a child. Even now I could understand why, at first glance, you might write him off as a grumpy old prick. I didn't know it at the time, but it was Gerry dressed as Santa Claus the year I flat out refused to hop on Santa's lap. I'd been rehearsing my proclamation of impeccable virtue and preparing to recite my well-rehearsed Christmas wish list. But the moment I saw Santa, I lost it – throwing a tantrum and refusing to make my in-person request. Instead, I remember crossing my fingers extra hard on the journey home and hoping my letter to the North Pole would be enough to convince Big Red I deserved to be well rewarded.

Momentarily put out, Nora was quick to recover. 'Well then, looks like I have you all to myself tomorrow, young Mr Fenwick.' She paused, as if a thought had just come to her. 'Probably best to keep your lovers separate, anyway. I hate to think what might happen if we had to compete for your affections. I am perhaps a little more mature than your other paramour. In general, I am averse to admitting such a thing, but in this instance I think it's an asset. I expect I am somewhat more cool-headed as an experienced woman of the world, so can share a man without being overwhelmed by the green-eyed monster. It would be hypocritical of me to have such counterproductive feelings when I also do not restrict myself to one suitor.'

It seemed Nora's campaign to lure me to her bed was far from over. And neither had her determination to rid herself of any love-rivals diminished, despite her words to the contrary. I maintained a polite grimace, not trusting myself to respond.

'Anything else, Nora?' Desmond said, staring down my unabashed admirer with impatience. 'Or are you *quite* done?'

Nora quirked a cheeky smirk and shrugged – she would speak whenever she pleased and there was nothing anyone could do about it.

Desmond must have realised this was as good as he'd get, so he continued. 'Our esteemed Dictator – hah, slip of the old tongue.' He chuckled to himself. 'Our esteemed *Director* took some convincing in approving this outing. We all know how hard-nosed our dear Ms Myles can be, but even she could not help but succumb to my faultless reasoning and relentless charm.'

Nora scoffed.

Desmond spoke louder, 'She did, however, insist I pass on this.' He reached into his trousers—

Nora wailed. 'Nobody wants to see that wrinkled old thing!'

He grumbled as he pulled a slip of paper from his pocket and cleared his throat with more fanfare than I expected was strictly necessary. 'Ms Myles requests attendees wear comfortable shoes and a jacket, bring a bottle of water and a travel mug or coffee flask—'

'What about lunch?' Nora said.

'—but there's no need to bring food as the kitchens will prepare lunch,' Desmond said, pointedly ignoring Nora as he shoved the paper back into his pocket, then smiled. 'Don't forget to eat your porridge tomorrow morning – you'll be needing the energy. And I promise you'll be getting some real *bang* for your *buck*.'

Desmond grinned like the cat that got the cream and headed for his seat, apparently having forgotten why he'd come up in the first place.

'Desmond,' I said, calling after him. 'Don't forget your prize.' Turns out the old scoundrel's win was legitimate – this time, anyway. I handed over his winnings: a selection of biscuits in a round tin with pastoral scenes shown on the sides and the lid.

He looked at his prize, appearing reluctant. I could understand the reaction. It was the kind of gift a parent might buy on behalf of their child to gift their grandfather on Father's Day, along with the card lovingly crafted at kindergarten. One could appreciate the effort put into making the card – 'Such interesting colour choices, my boy. And you've certainly used a substantial amount of glue – this painted macaroni won't be coming off anytime soon, will it? Well done.' But no one *actually* enjoyed those nasty, dry biscuits – did they? Not when you could buy a far superior biscuit from the supermarket for a fraction of the price. And what was one to do with yet *another* tacky biscuit tin? There were only so many sewing kits one household could contain. Most likely it'd be stacked on the ever-growing pile under the stairs or in the garage... It's the thought that counts though, right? But let's be honest, they could've thought of something else.

That's when I saw Desmond's expression slowly shift from dubious to delighted. He reached to claim his prize and said, 'This will do perfectly, I think. I have just the job in mind for this handsome tin.'

Suspicious... I almost tried to take it back, knowing he couldn't possibly be up to any good with a reaction like that. I returned the balls to the cage as Desmond returned to his seat and tried not to worry about his scheming.

Perhaps I could see Maud about one of those pills to calm myself for tomorrow? No, better not – they were potent little beasts. I couldn't be falling asleep on the coach – who knows what might become of me.

'OK,' I said, cutting across the hushed conversations which had broken out around the room. 'Next up we have a game of Two Lines – you know the rules. And the prize for this round is a lovely bottle of port.'

A flurry of excitement met this news, and I noticed Charles and Nora were now looking particularly determined. 'All right, folks' – I clapped my hands once – 'eyes down.'

The roomful of pensioners hunched over their tables, laser-focused as I opened the cage to grab the first ball.

'13, unlucky for some. 13.' Gladys gave her ticket a

triumphant yet vicious dab – seems she wanted the tipple too and was off to a good start. Otherwise, the room was filled with frustrated murmurs, everyone else disappointed to miss that auspicious first call. Though, it was a rather ominous ball to pull at the outset.

'32, buckle my shoe. 32.' Dabbers remained hovering over tickets to a susurration of tuts – another uncommon number this round it seemed.

'25, duck and dive. 25.' I saw several satisfied jabs – redemption! Perhaps this game might go their way after all.

'17, dancing queen. 17.' At this I heard a few cheers, an 'Oh, yeah!' and a 'Mamma Mia!' Sounds like we were back on track.

Then I pulled out the next ball… and winced.

Perhaps the punters would be too wrapped up in ABBA and wouldn't notice if I sneaked this ball back in? It was absolutely against the rules, but I think I would be forgiven in this instance… thanked, even. About to make my move, Charles – always the gentlemen, but much too observant – innocently enquired about the next number. There was nothing for it, I had to do it…

'85, staying alive. 85.'

Right on cue, Desmond was back out of his seat for the second time tonight – and tap-tap-tapping a rhythm on Gerry's near-bald head. The gruff old softy was trying to bat his fellow resident away when Desmond slid into the aisle and swaggered towards me at the front. He crooned in falsetto the opening lines to the Bee Gees hit as he strutted – as much as an octogenarian can – around the punters, blowing air-kisses to the ladies and nodding to the gents. He hit the chorus with even more gusto – nobody on the Sunset Villas grounds in any doubt about Desmond's intention to be staying alive.

Inside I was groaning, but I played along, pretending to be amused. He'd made a full lap of the room – treating each and every attendee to a little personal boogie and a line or two of the classic disco tune – before he settled back down in his seat.

'Thank you, Dez. That was a treat, as always.' I could've changed the call – there's plenty that rhymes with 'five' – but Desmond was liable to launch a one-man riot if he missed his moment in the spotlight.

'My pleasure, young man,' he said, breathless from exertion as he eased himself back into his seat. 'I'm not as spry as I once was, but I couldn't let down my fans.' His so-called fans were quick to shush the old troublemaker – they had a game to get on with.

I drew the next ball from the cage. '63, tickle me. 63.' Nora pursed her lips and gave me a wink. That woman was something else, any chance she got.

The next series of calls passed without incident – tension building and hands shaking with anticipation as dabbers marked out more numbers. A few contenders squirmed in their seats now – I suspected each were a single call away from victory.

'29, rise and shine. 29.'

'Bingo!'

Sure enough. Charles beamed as he rose, gracious in his acknowledgement of his fellow residents' polite applause. Gladys joined in the civilised round of congratulations, even though it was clear she'd had her heart set on that bottle of port. Nora, though – never shy to let her feelings be known – sat back with her arms crossed and a scowl plastered across her wrinkled face.

'Come now, Nora.' I wasn't willing to let her get away without a little ribbing, considering how much she dished out. 'I'm sure Charles will share a glass if you ask nicely.'

At that, she remembered herself, rearranging her face into her signature look of mischievous delight, which she turned on me. 'Such a cheeky young man. Were you not taught to respect your elders?' she said with eyebrows raised. 'What a naughty boy, I think I must discipline you myself. It would be irresponsible of me not to address this transgression. No, that would not do… I'll expect you in my apartment after bingo for your first lesson.'

I should've known better than to try and wind up Nora – that wily old girl could turn any situation to her advantage. Though fortune shone on me then in the form of Charles arriving with his alarmingly comical moustache to present his ticket and claim his prize. And so I was saved from concocting yet another excuse to escape Nora's proposition.

'This will do nicely, I think,' Charles said as he picked up his bottle of port and returned to his seat.

Our third and final game was uncharacteristically civilised, with Elspeth taking it out, announcing her triumph with somewhat more restraint and decorum than today's first two winners.

'Young Mr Fenwick, I do believe I have "bingo",' she said, making it clear she was only uttering such a foolish word as she was obliged to do so. She took her time raising herself from her seat, patting down her floral blouse and adjusting her already perfectly positioned pearls before making her way to the front.

Our highest-nosed resident placed her ticket on the table before clasping her hands together on her skirt to await my inspection.

'Mrs Abbington, you do indeed hold the winning ticket.' She nodded in affirmation, her blue rinse bouffant hair moving not an inch as she accepted her voucher. 'Your prize is a double pass to any of the local theatre company's matinee performances this season. I saw somewhere their next production is Macbeth, a modern interpretation set in the world of property investment.'

'Out, damned spot! Out, I say!' Nora projected her voice as she wrung her hands.

'That which hath made them drunk hath made me bold,' Desmond said, up and out of his seat once more, flailing an arm theatrically. 'What hath quenched them hath given me fire.'

'Fair is foul, and foul is fair,' Nora said, continuing to pluck random lines from the play to throw at her opponent.

'Knock, knock, knock!' Desmond rapped on the table. 'Who's there, in the name of Beelzebub?'

'There's daggers in men's smiles,' Nora said. Neither were making any sense, but both refused to concede defeat by being the first to miss coming back with a quote.

Elspeth, having had enough of such nonsense, attempted to return to her seat and distance herself from this faux intellectual exchange. Desmond threw up his arms in alarm as he stepped to block her path. 'Something wicked this way comes,' he said, pleased with himself for remembering a line with any relevance to the situation.

Elspeth stopped dead, pursed her lips and responded in a slow and measured manner, 'Blood will have blood.'

A collective gasp went up and Desmond was floored for a moment before he said, 'How now, you secret, black, and midnight hag!'

The accused hag narrowed her eyes, drawing in a deep

breath as she stepped right up in front of Desmond. Her voice low and menacing, she said, 'Double, double toil and trouble; fire burn and cauldron bubble. Cool it with a *baboon's* blood, then the charm is firm and good.' Her emphasis on baboon made it clear to whom she was referring.

Desmond stood, slack-jawed, unable to form a response – as stunned as the rest of us. Nora started a clap, which was soon picked up by everyone else in the room. Our resident rascal recovered and soon was beaming as he turned to allow Elspeth past, nodding in acknowledgement of a worthy opponent.

Elspeth tried her best to mask her pleasure, but there were limits to even her composure, a small smirk of delight escaping as she took her seat.

'Well, on that bombshell,' I said once the room had calmed down a little, 'that's all for tonight, folks. And I guess I'll be seeing you tomorrow bright and early for Desmond's mystery outing.'

With tonight's activity completed to everyone's satisfaction, the Sunset Villas' elderly residents packed up their personal dabbers and ambled out of the hall with the promise of tea, biscuits, and late-night news in the TV lounge.

Barry, my old mentor, paused a moment to give me a supportive thumbs up – always appreciated – then made his way out with the rest, his progress painfully slow.

Nora caught my eye with a wink and an air-kiss as I packed away the bingo balls. She was always good fun, but sometimes hard work too. I wouldn't have her any other way, but I had some low-level anxiety about what she might try tomorrow.

Then I noticed another of my favourites making her way towards my table as I finished up.

'I'm sorry I couldn't rig the game to get you that nice bottle of port,' I said, glad to have Gladys' more stereotypical grandmotherly presence after such a turbulent bingo night.

'Don't you worry about that, my boy,' she said, waving away the comment. 'I was just coming over to say how pleased I am that you've found someone special. We all are, and I'm sure your grandmother would have been too.'

'Oh, thanks Gladys,' I said, after a moment of trouble getting the words out. 'I'm… Yeah, I'm pretty excited—'

'And we appreciate your wish to have your privacy respected,' she said, steamrolling over what I had to say – not that I knew yet what it was I had to say. 'But, you see… we haven't got much time left, us oldies. We could drop off at any minute. I mean, I don't like to say it, but Barry is practically on death's door – you saw him tonight, I'm sure. You two spent a lot of time together when you were younger whenever you came to visit your Nana. Why, he's the one who got you into calling the bingo for us, and he's almost too frail to make it out of his room by himself anymore. Do you see?'

I sat in silence, astonished that Gladys could – or would! – guilt me so hard. Not the benign little old granny I'd always thought I'd known. She was really turning the screw here.

'There's no good holding anything back, my dear,' she said, continuing when she found me unresponsive. 'You wouldn't want to regret not including us – giving us the joy of young love – would you? You've been holding out on us for two weeks now. Every day counts when you get to our age.'

She was right. These people were some of my oldest – in both meanings of the word – friends. And I would be introducing them to someone who was becoming increasingly important to me, even over such a short period. I mean, we'd already committed to attending Richard and Lucy's wedding together – this was getting serious. It wasn't just that, though. My friends at the Sunset Villas retirement home would be expecting me to turn up with a lovely lady on my arm – all very old-fashioned and traditional. To be fair to them, I'd done nothing to disabuse them of that notion. And I didn't want to give them a heart attack turning up with Gabriel on my arm – gorgeous, but very much not a lady. I couldn't jeopardise my relationship with these people—

Here I went – again! – making excuses for myself. Coming out to my mates hadn't gone at all as I'd planned, but it had been so much better. Who's to say this won't be the same? And what had made me think coming out would be a one-time deal? I was quickly coming to realise it was an ongoing process, something I'd have to do over and over and over.

'Perhaps another time, Gladys,' I said, not mentally prepared to have this conversation right now.

I watched her wrinkled face fall.

'All right, dear.' She patted my hand before following the others out of the makeshift bingo hall.

I felt wretched, watching as the room emptied.

'Wimp,' I mumbled to myself.

# Chapter 2
# That's the best you've got?

**GABRIEL**

'So, who is it we're meeting again?' Theo said, clomping down the street on his crutches.

Claire sighed – she'd told us yesterday, and she'd told us again before leaving the flat. If I'm being honest, I was more surprised that she'd expected anything to register with Theo before he'd been told three times, minimum. 'We're meeting my nursing friends who—'

'Why do you have nursing friends?'

'Why would I *not* have nursing friends?' Claire said, not only annoyed but confused now as well.

'Uh, because you're not a nurse.'

After a pause, she asked, 'Are you a geologist?'

'What? No, obviously.' Theo was thrown by Claire's abrupt shift.

'Am I an artist?' she continued, raising an eyebrow.

'Well' – Theo made a show of thinking for a moment – 'you are a work of art – does that count?'

'Nice try. And would you consider yourself an architect?' she said, nodding towards me.

'Absolutely not.' He sounded offended. 'An artist does not limit oneself as an architect must – I laugh in the face of gravity.'

'And good taste,' I said, letting slip before I could stop myself.

Theo treated me to his most potent side-eye.

'Behave, children.' Claire slapped us both on the shoulder. 'What I'm trying to say is that we are not defined by what we do, and despite our vastly different professions we are all *dear* friends – are we not?'

'Doubtful,' Theo said, still smarting from my shady comment.

'And so, I reiterate: why can't I have nursing friends?'

'Fine! Yes, OK. Whatever. Probably for the best, having some medical professionals around – you know, considering my condition,' he said, gesturing to his foot in a cast.

'Yes, yes. You broke your bloody leg. How could we forget?' I said, unable to help myself from rolling my eyes.

'Hoo, boy. You all right, mate?' Theo had come to a stop to stare at me.

'No. You won't bloody shut up about your bloody leg,' I said, fed up – if he wanted to know, I'd tell him. 'Using your injury – which was your own idiotic fault, let's not forget – to get out of doing anything and everything. Fine, understandable that you can't mop, or vacuum, or take the rubbish out. But the incessant pleas from the couch are out of control: turn the heating up, pass my phone, open the window, refill my water glass, close the window, pass my computer, turn the heating down, make me a coffee, the list goes on.'

I liked to think of myself as a fairly relaxed person, in control. But lately, I just wanted to explode. I couldn't remember why I'd agreed to come out tonight…

That's not true, though. I'd come here, like so many others before me, for the big city life: doing new things, meeting new people, making new friends. There was little point being here if I was going to fester in the flat like one of Theo's unwashed socks down the back of the couch.

I'd fled my claustrophobia-inducing wee hometown for a reason – having done everything and gone as far as I could. I wasn't about to marry a nice girl and start popping out the kids – ding ding, next life stage – so what could I do next? Never mind the reality that if I wasn't already related to someone, I probably had their sister in my class at school, or played football with their son. Everyone knew everyone, and—

'Got that out of your system, did you? Feeling better now?' Theo said, pulling me back from my thoughts.

I was about to bite his head off when he raised his hands in surrender, lifting the crutches up in the process.

'I concede I may have hammed up the demands a bit—'

'A bit?' I said, incredulous.

'OK, a lot. In future I promise to get off my ass as required and only summon my slaves when absolutely necessary.'

'Fine.'

'Good.'

We'd been walking for a few minutes in tense silence when Claire said, 'You sure there's nothing else going on, Gabriel?'

'What? No.' What was she talking about?

23

'Not on edge because you're missing a certain someone? Frustrated that you won't get to see him for an *entire week*?'

No comment.

'But also nervous that it's all happening so fast, out of your control? Not even three weeks in, and you're being whisked away to attend one of his best friends' weddings as "the boyfriend"? How conflicted you must feel.'

I didn't dare to respond or react – her words like repeated blows to the head.

We kept walking, Claire and I keeping pace with Theo's ungainly swinging step.

What made me think I could get anything past that girl? And how had she distilled my swirling, chaotic thoughts into a mere few sentences?

'Sounds like tonight's light entertainment is just the distraction Gramps needs,' Theo said.

I almost snapped again, then realised he was probably right – not that I'd admit it.

'Oh, yes?' I said. 'Because an evening out went so well last time.' There was no venom in it, though. Claire's shrewd summary had been like a lance to my distracted and uncertain mood.

'Hey, it all worked out! Even if I'm a little the worse for wear.' Theo rapped on his cast. 'But, as I was saying before, it will be good to have the nurses around this evening – some medical professionals on hand in case I decide to proclaim my undying love yet again.' He made sucky-kissy noises at Claire.

'Nothing says "I love you" quite like a second broken limb,' I said with a small smile, having recovered some of my humour. I couldn't help myself – if I had to endure Theo's theatrics and the turbulence of this unfathomable pairing, at least I'd have fun with it.

'Don't you dare climb onto the bar,' Claire said, batting away Theo's affections, eyes wide and finger in his face. 'Are you listening? Repeat after me: I will not scale the furniture.'

'Yes, fine. I do solemnly swear that I will sit like a big boy.'

'Close enough,' Claire said, sighing for the second time in as many minutes.

'And you' – she swung her accusatory finger to focus on me – 'you should know better, Gramps. Don't encourage him.'

'Hey, he's your responsibility now.' I held my hands up. 'You broke him, you bought him.'

'I did not. He broke himself, the idiot.'

'A small price to pay.' Theo somehow still looked smug, despite the evident collateral damage. 'Worth it.'

I caught Claire's quick smile at that before she coached her features.

'We're here,' she said, stepping up to hold the pub door open for her newly minted boyfriend.

'Why, thank you! Such a gentleman,' Theo said, attempting a theatrical curtsy to Claire, fumbling over the front step and his crutches in the process before I could pull him upright again.

Claire took a calming breath. 'Just… get inside.'

I followed my flatmates into the pub. The reserved tables were already filling up, the weekly quiz doing its job bringing in the punters and their wallets on an otherwise sleepy Tuesday evening.

'Ah! The replacements have arrived – our saviours!' A stunning girl leapt from her bar stool and swept over, loose red curls framing a gorgeous face that seemed so pleased to see us.

'Hi Sam,' Claire said, embracing her friend. 'It's been much too long.'

'It has indeed… What's it been? One full week since we last laid eyes on each other?' Sam said, holding Claire at arm's length to get a good look at her. 'Separation on a timescale I can barely fathom.'

'Funny you say that, we were just discussing how long and distressing a week apart can be,' Claire said, smirking at me.

'Yes, just terrible,' Sam said. 'How are you, anyway, my sweet?'

'Better now that we're here. The children were fighting and I am in dire need of a drink,' Claire said, the long-suffering mother of two.

'They look perfectly well-behaved to me,' Sam said, turning her attention to me and Theo. 'But you didn't tell me they were both so handsome – how delightfully distracting!' She wrapped us both in a tight hug – somehow managing to keep Theo upright in the process – and planted a kiss on our cheeks.

'I'm Sam, by the way.' She settled back on her stool to take a sip from her near-full pint and gestured to four other untouched drinks. 'I just grabbed these. Didn't know what you liked, so I took a stab. This quiz is important brain work, and I can't have you dehydrated – we need those brain cells nice and lubricated.'

'Thanks Sam,' I said, feeling my face pull into a smile. Her enthusiasm was infectious, and I was enjoying myself already.

'That's no trouble, my sweet. Next round is yours – Oh! Here he is… speaking of nice and lubricated, our other regular team member returneth from the privy.'

I turned to see someone approaching our table, with a face I knew but couldn't immediately place.

Sam shot out her hands to present the newcomer. 'And this dashing specimen is—'

'Cameron,' I said, recognising the smile.

'Ho ho ho, they've already met,' Sam said. 'Well, this just got *much* more interesting.'

'It's not like that,' he said, smiling wider as he pulled up a stool and grabbed the final full pint, 'unfortunately.'

'Pity. You two would produce such stunning gaybies,' Sam said, tutting in disappointment.

'Cameron looked after Theo when he broke his leg,' I said. He wore that same smile he'd offered at the hospital – nice and reassuring. I hardly recognised him out of his scrubs, but the bigger change was the way he held himself. Tonight he looked fresh and relaxed, not as if his soul had been crushed under the unending stream of drunken injuries pouring through his night shift at the emergency department.

'Nice to meet you,' Theo said, looking sheepish as he shook his hand. 'I can't say it's nice to see you *again* because I don't recall the first time.'

'I'm not surprised,' Cameron said, laughing. 'But I'm glad to see you up and about – just please don't break anything tonight, I'm off duty.'

'Now that sounds like something I've heard before, too,' Theo said. 'Mere minutes ago, in fact.'

'It's good to see you again.' I ignored Theo to shake Cameron's hand – which seemed more appropriate now in the pub than it had during our awkward interaction at the hospital.

'You too,' Cameron said, still smiling. Then, looking around at the assembled team, he said, 'So, what're we going to call ourselves?'

'Yes!' Sam said. 'Team names, what have we got?'

'I thought you came every week?' I said.

'Of course. Not going to leave our crown undefended, are we Cameron?' Sam said, glowing with pride.

'Not a chance,' he said. 'Not even with our bride-to-be absent.'

'But... don't regular teams have a regular name they recycle every week? For notoriety, or bragging rights, or whatever?'

'True, most do. But coming up with a new team name is part of the fun, right? Why would we starve ourselves of that?' Cameron said.

'It helps us fly under the radar, too,' Sam said, leaning in.

'The other teams don't recognise the name and so they underestimate us,' Cameron said. 'It plays in our favour.'

'If they knew so many of the winning teams of the past were in fact the various incarnations of a single team, they might—'

'We're hardly incognito' – Cameron shrugged – 'they should recognise us by now.'

'True,' Sam said. 'And anyway, this week we've switched up the players.'

'So we definitely need a shiny new name for our shiny new team,' added Cameron.

'Cameron is our token testosterone,' Sam said. 'You know, for diversity. Can't have a team stacked with only brilliant women – got to give the other teams a sporting chance. But tonight, we've got three – three! – paragons of masculinity.'

'It's OK,' Claire said. 'I'm sure we'll manage.'

'Yes, if they're no good on the quiz…' Sam scrutinised me, Theo, and Cameron. 'At least they're nice to look at.'

'I'm glad we could provide a service,' Cameron said, 'but I fear our beauty may be distracting. How will you work under such conditions?'

Sam burst out with laughter. 'Oh, my dear. As Claire said, I'm sure we'll manage,' she said, winking as she patted Cameron on the arm. 'Now, we need a name. Just remember, we're a classy crew, not amateurs. So there'll be no quizzing on this or that nonsense.'

'What?' Theo said, smirking. 'Like "Quiz In My Pants"?'

'"Quiz On Your Face".'

'"Pens Out, Don't Quiz Inside".'

'Exactly,' Sam said. 'Basic. Overdone. Vulgar. We can do so much better.'

'What do the other teams go with?' I said.

'See them over there?' Sam pointed to what looked like a gaggle of middle-aged shop assistants from the homeware department. 'They've been "Let's Get Quizzical" since before we started coming here. Yawn.'

'And those guys behind me?' Cameron nodded his head back to a loud bunch of finance lads. 'They're "Our Drinking Team Has a Trivia Problem".'

A collective groan.

'What about something nursing-related,' I said, 'considering the team's usually made up of nurses?'

'And a geologist,' Claire said.

'Geology *student*, let's not get ahead of ourselves,' Theo said, the cheeky prick pushing his luck.

'Yes, yes,' I said, interrupting before they both got stuck

in. 'I was thinking "Nurse Ratched"? She's a formidable foe – that'll give the other teams the chills.'

'Oh, that's *good*,' Claire said, distracted from the act of smacking Theo around the head. 'But – but how about we dial it up a bit... Something – something like "Nurse Ratched and the Orderlies".' She gestured around our team, her eyes glowing as she looked at each of us with manic glee. 'That'll give them a fright.'

'Or "Nurse Ratched and the Shock Therapists"?' I said, racking my brain for references from the film adaptation I hadn't seen since we'd studied it at school.

'Yes, yes! Turn it up – now we're cooking,' Claire said, loving the idea. Sam and Cameron – real life nurses – however, remained dubious.

'"Nurse Ratched and the Lobotomists"?' I said, then immediately thought better of it. 'Perhaps that's a bit much—'

'That's the one,' Claire said with finality, nodding as her grin widened. 'That'll fair put the shits up the others.'

'Not exactly what we like to associate with our profession,' Cameron said, though he looked amused.

'It's got punch, though, doesn't it?' Sam was coming around to the idea. 'Authoritative. Ruthless. I like it.'

'Let's do it,' Cameron said, smiling as he shrugged. '"Nurse Ratched and the Lobotomists".'

\*\*\*

We were on our second drink when the quizmaster kicked things off. He rattled through the team names – Sam and Cameron had been spot on about the other regulars – and our team was treated to a few gasps from around the room when he announced our ominous name.

Sam, Cameron, and Claire were quick to prove we deserved it, dominating round after round.

History: 1750s this, Queen that, War of the Whatever. Geography: hang on… were they sure these places weren't fictional? General knowledge: OK, now how could anyone be expected to know these things?

Theo and I helped on a couple of questions, but were otherwise left to sip our drinks and 'look pretty' as Sam put it at one point. Theo took the compliment, framing his face to pose for an imaginary photo shoot. I rankled at the comment but had to admit she had a point.

I didn't object too much because – despite feeling like a bit of an idiot – I was having a great time. And no, I wasn't thinking about Arthur – he'd be with the oldies at bingo about now – or how long it'd be till I'd see him again – not till his friend's wedding.

Well, shit. I was thinking about him now, wasn't I?

So, I could already tell this thing with Arthur was something else – not your usual one-night stand or two week flame and fizzle. And now that I'd had a taste, I wanted more – much more.

A week's separation might not sound like much in the wider scheme, but when you're picking up speed, excited to be building momentum, then you're slamming on the brakes for a week. It felt hollow – like your favourite new toy had been put out of reach on the top shelf until you'd cooled your jets.

But why were we doing this to ourselves? We both had our regular commitments and things already in the calendar before we ran into each other, and before this last-minute wedding appeared.

As one of the Best Men, Arthur had additional pre-wedding duties, including a stag do Richard was bound to demand despite the tight timeframe.

Our short-term schedules were stacked, and neither of us could abandon all that. Just because we were busy sweeping each other off our respective feet didn't mean we should sweep everything else in our lives away too.

Not only was this approach the mature, adult thing to do, I don't think I'd have it any other way. I couldn't start what might develop into something real with someone who drops everything important in their life the moment a bit of tail flashes in his face.

Though, I did like to think I was a worthy bit of tail.

Anyway, with all that going on, it left little time for 'The Arthur and Gabriel Show' – which was especially galling when he'd just asked me to be his boyfriend. I know, I know – bleurgh – what a sop-fest. Don't need to label things to get excited about getting to know each other. Even so, it's a milestone. And to have just arrived, then have to forget about it. What a rollercoaster.

I mean, we have phones, so I should just stop being so dramatic? But let's be real: calls and messages don't cut it. Not when what we really wanted was to get hands-on again, you know, get right down to—

'Gramps.' Theo dropped a fresh pint in front of me and waved a hand in my face. 'Mate, we lost you there – again.'

'Sorry, I checked out for a minute there.' I felt myself flushing with embarrassment. 'What did – uh – what did I miss?'

'Well, it's good to have you back.' Sam smiled as I dragged my mind back to our table. 'What could possibly have captivated our fair Gabriel more than eighties pop culture?'

'He was thinking about sword fights with King Arthur, weren't you, Gramps?' Theo said, making steel clashing noises and laughing at his own joke.

'Very dangerous,' Claire said. 'We mustn't distract him or he might get *impaled* by the imaginary Arthur.'

Theo hooted and gave his girlfriend a high-five.

'I can understand why that might be distracting,' Cameron said, delighted by my discomfort.

'Oh yes. I mean, I love my Whitney and Madonna trivia' – Sam nodded in understanding – 'but when you've got dick on the brain, there's no helping you.'

'All right! Yes, thank you for your thoughts, everyone. Lesson learnt,' I said, hands held up. 'I'm paying attention.'

'Well, that's great to hear,' Sam said, 'but it's the interval now. We're halfway through, time for more drinks and a toilet break.'

'Yes, so we've got plenty of time to hear more about this legendary clash,' Cameron said, sipping his pint.

'Oh, break time – must be my round?' I said, dropping down from my stool. 'I'll go get us drinks.'

'Just did that, Gramps,' Theo said. 'You're not getting away so easily.'

'Ah,' I said, looking at the near-full glass Cameron had just sipped from, then at the table with fresh pints in front of the rest of us.

I climbed back onto my stool. 'Or – actually – uh, there was something I meant to ask before,' I said, attempting to deploy diversionary tactics Plan B. 'Who's your usual fourth team member?'

Sam raised an eyebrow. 'That's the best you've got?'

'Pretty weak as far as deflections go,' added Cameron.

'I'll bite,' Sam said, 'because I adore talking about our lovely Lucy, and I think we've made you squirm enough.' She beamed at me before continuing, 'Our Lucy is busy with wedding planning this week. I should be helping, but there's only so much flower and lace chat a girl can handle – I gave myself the night off. It's all been very short notice. She proposed to her boneheaded boyfriend last week – don't ask me what she sees in him, loves him to bits though. Wedding's this Saturday – would you believe it? Not even two weeks after she popped the question!'

'This Saturday?' This was all sounding suspiciously familiar…

'Yes! Crazy, right? I'm sure this would've raised a few eyebrows amongst the aunties, they'll certainly be looking for any signs of a bump to explain this *rather* brief engagement,' she said with pursed lips and a conspiratorial air. 'Anyway, our Lucy is gorgeous and full of random facts. And as wonderful and welcome as you boys are, we're looking forward to having her back too – you know, because she knows some of the answers.'

Ignoring the good-natured dig, I had to be sure. 'So, what's the husband-to-be's name?'

'Richard Singh,' Sam said, then turned to Cameron. 'And he's got those two mates of his as his Best Men – what were their names?'

'Jared and – who was the other one?' Cameron said.

'Arthur,' I said.

'Yes, that's the one!' Sam said. 'What? How'd you know?'

'Hang on,' Claire said, holding her hand out. 'Gabriel, are we talking about *your* Arthur? Lucy's future best friend-in-law is *your* Arthur?'

'Ah, yeah.'

'Fuck me,' Theo said. 'Small world.'

I took a gulp from my pint. So much for escaping that small town life, you know, where everyone knows everyone. 'It sure is.'

# Chapter 3
# Why have we got such a big coach?

**ARTHUR**

My elderly friends were milling around the Sunset Villas reception area when I arrived. They were busy speculating about where we might be headed today, travel mugs in hand. I spotted Gerry, Gladys, Nora, Charles, Elspeth, Maud, and a bunch of others I didn't recognise – not bingo players or Nana's friends. Desmond had remained tight-lipped, which only fuelled the excitement and anticipation, each guess wilder than the last.

'Good to see you, lad.' Desmond stepped in beside me, clapping me on the shoulder and looking up the driveway. 'Now, where's this bloody coach of ours?' He was distracted – I wondered if the pressure of pulling off an unforgettable day was getting to our otherwise easy-going octogenarian. His own fault, really. He'd talked up this day and couldn't fail before we'd even left the retirement home.

It was five minutes till nine when a huge coach pulled into the double-height covered parking bay outside reception, a few faces on board peering out. The elderly adventurers flooded out to meet the coach in one mass shuffle.

'About bloody time,' Desmond said, battling to get around the herd. 'Supposed to be here half an hour ago!'

At first I didn't understand the issue – they weren't scheduled to depart until nine – but then the embarking procedure began...

The coach driver – sporting a tweed flat cap and all – left the engine running and clambered down the stairs. He set a portable step on the pavement before greeting the most eager resident at the front of the spontaneously formed queue.

I watched as he held their belongings – handbags, travel mugs, canes, walking frames – and helped them onto the step. Next, he guided their hands to the handrail and ghosted them up the stairs – ready to catch if anyone tilted backwards as they navigated the steep ascent. Then, safely aboard, he'd hand back their possessions before repeating the whole procedure with the next resident.

It was excruciating.

Desmond was huffing and puffing, stalking in and out of the reception area, frowning at his watch every ten seconds or so. I headed over to help speed things along so Desmond didn't erupt, but despite the vast size of the coach, its doorway was too narrow for me to be of any use.

'This coach is bigger than the usual, isn't it?' I said while I waited with Desmond, attempting to distract him from his schedule with other coach-related enquiries.

'What's that you said, lad?' he said, tapping his earlobe.

'Speak up, you know the old hearing's not the sharpest.'

'Why have we got such a big coach?' I spoke a little louder over the sound of the engine. 'It's different to the one Brenda normally organises for your outings, isn't it?'

'I wanted to keep her involvement to a minimum, my boy.' He kept his conspiratorial whisper as quiet as he could, but it was still louder than most. 'My prize was being in charge of this day, so can't be conceding any parts of the organising. If I gave our dear Director an inch, she'd take a mile, you see. The more I could organise myself, the less influence she'd have.' He winked at me.

'How'd you get this coach, then?'

'With difficulty...' His already wrinkled face creased further in consternation. 'A necessary evil, though. My daughter's a member of some Garden Club that helps plant parks and waterways and suchlike. They visit stately gardens, too – not unlike our usual uninspiring outings. Now, you see, my daughter's bothersome friend runs this Garden Club, and her husband drives the coach.' Desmond pointed his chin towards the man under the flat cap who was still valiantly shepherding the elderly onto the coach. 'I was put in touch with this friend of my daughter's. This friend made a big song and dance about using their coach but eventually agreed to let us have it – on two conditions,' Desmond said, his bushy eyebrows shooting up. His face clearly said, 'Can you believe it?' which I knew he was going to hold until I asked the question. I mean, just tell your tale. I had to assume he made it interactive to ensure I was paying attention.

'What were the two—'

'First,' he said, cutting me off with a gnarled and callused index finger, 'she insisted on her Garden Club

38

members being invited along, on *our* outing.' He shook his head in outrage, then flung up a second sausage-finger. 'Then when she found out where we were going, she demanded a *minor* detour. "The residents will love it, too," she says. Some stately home with its manicured grounds and gardens. Not the direction I'd planned for my outing. But this woman's a real tough customer, I tell you.'

He glanced up to see that the Sunset Villas residents were almost all settled on the coach, only a few left to board.

'But luckily,' he said, relaxing back to his usual cunning self, 'only a handful of their members were available at such short notice – us geriatrics are still the majority. Power in numbers, my boy. And that garden visit of hers – fancy flowers and trimmed bushes – well, let's just say I have an idea or two about that.' He nodded to me with his signature sly grin as if it wasn't blatantly obvious that mischief was afoot.

Desmond and I headed over to the coach as the last of the residents conquered the great climb. He turned to me again, 'I must apologise, young man. In all the excitement I forgot to mention that this friend of my daughter has also brought along a niece of hers, a lovely filly by all accounts.' He gave me a nudge and a wink. 'I know, I know – you've already got yourself a bit of fluff on the go, but you're young, won't hurt to get to know this young lady a little better today too.'

I had to tell him – I had to tell them all. I couldn't let this go on.

I stopped at the base of the stairs and turned to Desmond. 'Actually, I'm – uh, the – uh, person I'm seeing is a – his name's Gabriel.'

There, I said it – eventually. I choked on the delivery,

unable to come straight out and say I'm gay, instead saying that I'm seeing a guy. Enough to get the message across, anyway.

'Gabrielle, what a magnificent name – so *exotic* sounding. I'll wager she's a real minx,' Desmond said, grinning like a scoundrel.

'No, not Gabrielle. His name's Gab—'

'Yes, yes. Don't you worry about that one. Not here, is she? Today, you'll have this niece to keep you entertained, my boy. Samantha, I think her name was – a much more down-to-earth name, but I'm sure she'll do you just fine. Go on, don't you hold up my schedule any more, get up there.'

I attempted to correct him again, but he wasn't hearing any of it. I'd even dropped any pretence at gender-neutral language, but he was either too hard of hearing, or too focused on getting us going that he didn't register what I was saying. He shoved me up the stairs and I fumbled, trying to get my feet back under me.

'Good to have you on board today, Arthur.' I looked up to see the pallid face of the man under the flat cap as he settled into the driver's seat.

'Mr Binfield – uh, what are you doing here?' I was too surprised at seeing my browbeaten neighbour, and still recovering from the shove, to come up with anything else. He was unrecognisable in tidy clothes – Patty always had him doing chores around their section, so his regular attire comprised overalls and tatty, faded cast-offs.

'I drive the coach for the Garden Club ladies' outings,' Philip Binfield said pleasantly, immune to my rude outburst. 'Thought I'd better take the reins again for today's extra outing. So good of the Club to invite the retirement home residents out for the day, isn't it?'

'That's not – I think you've got it the – I'm sure it'll be a nice day for the Club and the residents.' I realised almost too late I did not want to get myself in the middle of committee politics…

'Indeed, it will. For you too, I'm sure,' he said, a sheepish smile growing. 'Go on, Patty and Samantha will be waiting for you.'

My face fell as I finally made the connection. Desmond had mentioned earlier… The bothersome friend who ran the Garden Club, the husband driver, the special guest niece.

'There you are, my dear Arthur,' Patty said, effusing from a seat a couple of rows back. She was sitting next to another woman who looked vaguely familiar – or she just had that generic middle-aged white lady look about her – presumably another Garden Club member. And across the aisle—

'I've saved you a seat next to my niece, Samantha.' Patty gestured with obvious pride to the empty seat next to a gorgeous red-head. 'Now, you will thank me, I'm sure. I had to fend off several elderly gentlemen very interested in taking that space for themselves.'

As Patty spoke, I caught sight of vigorous waving from a few seats back. It was Nora – and was that a bottle of sherry? She left no room for misunderstanding her intentions: I was to sit next to her.

This was a lose-lose situation, but I knew what I had to do. I could apologise to Nora later, and she would use that as an opportunity to try and wrangle a promise or some kind of concession out of me. She was a shrewd operator, and willing to bide her time. Patty, on the other hand, would not let this drop until she'd seen it through. Better to get this over with now.

41

I made a face of apology to Nora before easing into the seat next to Patty's niece as the coach door swung shut and Philip got us underway.

'Uh, hi. I'm Arthur,' I said, turning to face the niece properly for the first time.

She responded to my tentative greeting with a deep, delighted laugh. 'Oh, my. Don't look so mortified, man. I'm not going to eat your heart, devour your soul, or whatever else it is you think I'm going to do.'

'I – I didn't think that.' How did I tell her I was worried about being foisted on some poor girl with romantic expectations, despite having zero interest in her? Not her specifically, just the female half of the population in general. And if I was being honest, the possibility of the girl being Patty 2.0 terrified me like nothing else could.

'Though, I can see why Aunty Pat was so desperate for me to meet you – you are a looker, aren't you?'

'Uh – thanks,' I said. 'You look nice too.'

She laughed again, then pursed her lips. 'Pretty face but not exactly sparkling conversation, are you? What's got you all tied up in knots?' she said, flicking her hair back. 'Is it my stunning good looks?'

She wasn't shy, and I could tell she would not be brushed off so easily. I just had to tell her why I wasn't interested – that'd put a pin in this whole sorry story. Coming out to a stranger ought to be easy. No real stakes – might even be for the best, getting Patty off my case. 'No, it's not that. I—'

'My imposing personality? I have been told I come on a bit strong sometimes.'

'No, no—'

'It can be intimidating to men. Emasculating – like a

42

vibrant pink nail file slowly grinding against their delicate manhood.'

I winced at the thought. 'It's not that, I'm—'

'Oh.' She looked me up and down, pursing her lips again and nodding with eyes wide. 'I see.'

'I'm gay.' I heard the words spill out. And said in such a way that it sounded like I was sorry to be letting her down, resigned to having been caught out.

'Yes, you are. Obviously,' she said, throwing her hands up in faux frustration. 'There's no need to be so sad about it – it's perfectly normal, "Born This Way" and all that.'

'That's not the—'

'Plus,' she said, jabbing me in the chest, 'it's going to be a long day for both of us if you insist on moping through it.'

'I'm not sad, just a bit overwhelmed,' I admitted. She was a hurricane, my admission ripped from me almost against my will.

'Oh, I'm sorry,' she said. 'But considering my Aunty Pat's tried to set us up, I presume she's not aware of this situation? Meaning you haven't yet fully embraced the gay? And there I go, plunging your deepest, darkest secrets!' She grabbed my chin to look me in the eye. 'But how could I have missed it? You're *so* gay.'

'Wow – um – thanks?'

'Perhaps I've become desensitised?' she said before releasing me again. 'I had a wonderful time last night with a couple of gays – all that gayness flying around has temporarily blinded me to yours.'

I saw my opening. Having recovered from Samantha's verbal onslaught, it was time to regain a little ground in this conversation. 'A *wonderful* time with a couple of gays, was it? And what were you lot up to, hmm?' I said, waggling my eyebrows.

Samantha turned to me, open-mouthed for a moment before a grin spread across her face. 'It's alive.' She lifted her arms and her voice in triumph. 'It's alive!'

Rude. I like to think I'm not so vain, but I'm sure I'm easier on the eyes than Frankenstein's monster. 'Dodging the question? Were you watching from the sidelines? Too embarrassed to admit that's how you get your kicks?'

She smiled wider still. 'Maybe today won't be so dull after all…' she said.

***

Turns out Samantha wasn't anything like Patty had led me to fear – that is, a younger version of herself. Samantha was animated and enthusiastic, worked as a nurse at the hospital we'd taken Theo to after he caned himself, and she preferred to go by Sam.

Picking up on an argument we overheard further down the coach, we too were now debating whether jam or cream went on scones first. I was highlighting the merits of the jam-first approach – which is the correct way, for your information – when Patty leapt up to announce we were less than ten minutes away, so could we all please ready ourselves.

Desmond wouldn't like that, not one bit. He was a man of a certain age who wouldn't be told what to do, especially not on his big day. But he was a big boy – I didn't need to intervene, couldn't spend all day distracting him whenever things didn't go his way.

Though, turns out I didn't need to as Nora soon swept up the aisle, bottle of sherry in hand, pouring out measures as she went.

Patty noticed too, bursting from her seat to charge down the aisle. 'You cannot drink on this coach! Put that away, right now.'

Nora finished pouring a measure for Charles and Elspeth, before turning to face my neighbour. She supported herself with one hand gripping a headrest, the other holding the bottle like she might knock it against the side of Patty's head if provoked.

'My dear Garden Club lady,' Nora said, achieving maximum condescension despite being a head shorter than the younger woman. 'I'm not sure if you're aware, but today is the anniversary of the passing of Arthur's grandmother, and our dear friend. Now, we are not a raucous hen or stag party turning your beloved coach into a party bus – we are commemorating a wonderful lady with a quiet moment of reflection while enjoying her favourite tipple. Would you care to join us?'

I watched in fascination as Patty was played with such aplomb. She attempted to swallow her outrage and accept a small pour. Yet, she was still unable to corral her features into anything better than a sucked-lemon grimace. Nora poured some for the woman next to Patty – I still couldn't figure out why she looked so familiar – who was delighted to see her friend shut down so comprehensively, but trying not to show it.

'Now, my delicious young man,' Nora said as she turned her back on the others, 'as you gifted this bottle to me, it's only fitting you should have a taste.' Her bingo prize from a couple weeks ago, of course. She must've given up hope of sharing the bottle with me, alone in her rooms.

'Have you got your travel mug?' she said, waggling the

45

bottle.

Nora poured me a measure, and I sipped my sherry which warmed my throat as it went down.

Nana's anniversary wasn't for a few weeks yet, but close enough for Nora's purposes. Some might be outraged on Nana's behalf at having her passing used in such a fashion, but I know she would have approved.

I think she would approve of Gabriel too. 'Whatever makes you happy, sweetheart.' That's what she would've said, always wanting the best for her grandbabies. But I didn't have to speculate – I had a coach full of my adopted grandparents, some who'd known me for over half my life, who only wanted the same as my Nana.

'Now, I see you've been glamoured by this young beauty,' Nora said. 'Seems I have my work cut out for me – a three-way battle for your affections now, is it? Or, we can share, if you prefer, Arthur?'

I was still stuttering a response to quash the obvious intrigue on Sam's face when she introduced herself to Nora.

The old woman poured a measure into my seat companion's cup too. 'I hate to dash your hopes young lady, but did this handsome scoundrel perhaps not mention that he is courting another?'

Sam arched an eyebrow. 'No, he did not.'

'Yes, it is true,' Nora said, her face a picture of regret. 'I hate to do this to you Arthur, but this beautiful young lady deserves to know that she's not the only horse in this race. That you are playing the field, as they say. Some women with more delicate sensibilities than I may object to being treated so. I, of course, understand the perils of pursuing a handsome cad such as yourself.' Nora turned her full attention onto Sam. 'I do hate to besmirch my dear Arthur's name, but I can't have him going around breaking all these girls' hearts – ghastly. I admit, telling you serves a dual purpose – the other being winnowing down the pool of candidates for his affections. I hope you won't judge him too harshly, I just wanted you to understand what you were getting yourself into.'

'I'll go easy on him,' Sam said, giving Nora a reassuring smile.

'That's good. Thank you, my dear. Nevertheless, I shouldn't worry, Arthur will soon come to realise nothing compares to the rich taste of a more *mature* fruit such as myself,' Nora said. She blew me a kiss before turning to continue towards the front of the coach.

I felt a presence boring into the side of my head and turned to find Sam staring at me, eyebrow raised. 'I have been wildly misled in the lead up to today.'

'What?'

'I've been primed by all Aunty Pat's husband-material propaganda. You are regularly referred to as "my handsome gentleman bachelor neighbour who never brings any girls home". So when she was pressing this meeting on me, I thought, at worst you'd be a troll. If that was the case, I could say as much to our unsolicited matchmaker, then I could forever put this issue to bed. And at best, you were everything Aunty Pat said you would be, and I could take *you* to bed instead. Either way, I wouldn't have to hear about you every time I saw her... Turns out you're something else entirely – gorgeous, but utterly useless to me and my lady bits. A pity.'

What was I supposed to say to that? 'Sorry?'

'What I'm trying to say is that I can understand keeping this from my Aunty Pat – I know how she likes to get her

47

beak in everybody's business. But the rest of these oldies' – Sam gestured around at everyone on the coach – 'aren't they your friends?'

'Yes,' I said, unable to prevent my shoulders from slumping slightly in shame.

'And, how do you feel about that?'

'I'm working on it, OK?'

'Can I presume this third paramour vying for your affections is—'

'A guy, yes.'

'And?'

'And we've only been dating for a couple weeks, but he's great,' I said, feeling my cheeks heat up at the same time despite my shame. 'Really, really great.'

'You know, if this relationship develops, you're going to want to tell—'

'I know! I know, I'm getting there.'

'So is Christmas,' she said, smirking at me.

'Shut up and drink your sherry.'

# Chapter 4
# What does he give you that I don't?

## GABRIEL

'Why haven't the ball baskets been refilled yet, Gabriel?' Murray said with his habitual passive aggressive hostility.

'Why haven't you left yet, Murray?' Sheela countered, sweeping around a corner from where our boss hadn't seen her.

Murray stuttered a moment before recovering. 'We've got a bus load coming in later – big group – if you'd checked the bookings you'd know that.' There he went, a desperate attempt to regain a little ground. 'They only called this morning. Lucky I could fit them in this afternoon. Anyway, as I said, I have to head off early – I trust you'll manage?' Said as if he believed the opposite.

'As we do every week, Murray,' Sheela said, the disdain thick as syrup.

He returned to his office, muttering under his breath

something about having a job done properly.

'Forget him, he'll be gone soon enough,' Sheela said to me. 'I brought snacks.'

'Yes! That's more like it. What have you got for us this week?'

'Millionaire's shortbread. Nothing too fancy, I'm afraid – not much more than butter, sugar, condensed milk, *more* butter, *more* sugar, and chocolate.'

'More is more.'

'So simple, though,' Sheela said, cracking open the lid on her home baking.

'Yet so delicious,' I said, already chewing on my first bite.

'I decided on something even our dear, vanilla manager would recognise. An olive branch, if you will. I'm wary of pushing him too far, can't have him going postal on us. But now he's stomped off in a huff so he's not getting any.'

'That's what he's like, though, isn't it?'

'Acting like he's been hard done by.'

'I'm sure he believes that, too.'

'Never mind him… As well as snacks, I come bearing news,' Sheela said, her eyes alight with excitement. 'Big news!'

'Go on,' I said, unable to help myself from smiling.

'My boy is getting married!'

'What? Congratulations! That's fantastic.' I was genuinely excited for my friend, but it felt like everyone was getting engaged this week… Not that I'd say such a thing to Sheela, wouldn't want to burst her bubble. 'I didn't realise either of your boys were so close to—'

'Neither did I,' Sheela said, laughing with delight. 'I don't think my dear Richie realised either. His girlfriend –

fiancé! – was the one who proposed.'

Another coincidence—

'I should've known, of course,' Sheela said. 'Lucy is a girl who knows what she wants, doesn't take any rubbish. It's what I admire about her, exactly what my Richie needs.'

'When – uh – when's the wedding?' I asked, as if I didn't already know.

'Saturday!' Sheela was practically jumping now. 'Three more sleeps until my baby is hitched.'

'OK, this is just ridiculous,' I said to myself. But how was I only now making the connection that Sheela's 'Richie' was Arthur's 'Richard'? I specifically left home to get away from this small town shit.

'It's all very last minute, I know, but Lucy locked in the venue after the previous booking was cancelled.'

'I've never heard of something so far fetched.' I was still muttering under my breath, not hearing a word Sheela said. 'Does *everyone* in this city know each other too, just like home, but on a grander scale?'

'What?' Sheela said.

'It's absurd! You couldn't write this nonsense,' I said, processing out loud and shaking my head. Can I not go anywhere? Smothered by relatives, everyone knowing my business all the time… I'd escaped my own suffocation, only to dive straight into someone else's—

A golf ball smacked into my chest and clattered to the floor.

'Wh—'

Another hit me in the stomach. I looked up to see Sheela, looking fierce, golf ball in hand.

'What are you—'

Sheela lobbed another, but I knocked it aside.

'Stop it!'

'You stop it! You're being a shit. What've you got stuck up your arse, hmm?' Sheela said, eyes wide, chucking another few balls at me. 'My boy's getting married and all you can say is how ridiculous it is! What's so bloody ridiculous? Why can't my boy get married?'

A bunch of men in office attire appeared at our reception desk – looks like they were knocking off early today, too. They were here most weeks – consultants of some sort – and their chat comprised a constant stream of gripes about colleagues and clients. Tedious, but I was still none the wiser as to what they actually *consulted* on.

Sheela took their payment, and I handed over their clubs and balls in silence.

Once they were in their usual bay, I turned back to Sheela, their timely interruption having given me a second to catch myself mid pity party. 'Ah, fuck,' I said, moving to hold Sheela's hands – ostensibly to express regret and show my earnestness, but in truth I just wanted to prevent any future golf ball assaults. Firstly, because it kind of hurt, but also because I didn't want my chest polka dotted with purple bruises.

'Just feeling a bit hemmed in. I thought I'd escaped all that when I came here,' I said. 'But that's no excuse, I'm sorry. I shouldn't have made it all about me.'

'It's not your style,' Sheela said, nodding in agreement with my assessment.

'I'm excited for the wedding' – I attempted a small, conciliatory smile – 'and I guess I'll see you there.'

'You will?' Sheela's frustration switched to surprise in an instant.

'Got the invite, didn't I?'

'You did? How'd you wrangle that?' She glowed with excitement now – after all, it was her boy's wedding, and this revelation only added to the anticipation. Another thing I loved about Sheela: she didn't hold a grudge.

'Well, I—'

'I mean, as much as I would've loved to invite you myself and bring you along with me, it'd be frowned upon, I suspect. You know, mother of the groom bringing along another man – a much younger man at that. Especially when I'm still married to – and unfathomably in love with, even after all these years – the father of the groom.'

She was rambling with enthusiasm now – no way I'd be getting a word in. Instead, I sneaked another slice of millionaire's shortbread while she was distracted.

'Hang on,' she said, levelling an accusing finger at me, eyes going wide again. 'Have you been cheating on me with my boy? I thought I was the only Singh in your life,' Sheela said, hand on chest.

I laughed. 'Don't worry, you're still the number one Singh in—'

'You're worthless! How dare you pander to me,' Sheela said with a smile, clobbering me with more golf balls. Even though now good-natured, it still hurt. 'What does he give you that I don't? He certainly doesn't bake. A good-looking boy, I'll admit, but he's got nothing on his dear mother.'

'That's very true, it's the other way around, actually – I was the one baking for Richard.'

'What? You baked for – no, go back, explain yourself,' Sheela said. 'Why were you baking for my Richie? How do you know my boy in the first place? And how did I not know about this? I'm his mother – I should know these things!'

'I met Richard, Jared, and Arthur right here, at the driving range, a couple weeks ago on my Sunday shift—'

'Of course he came on Sunday, knew his dear old mother wouldn't be working – cheeky sod.'

'Anyway, remember that's when Arthur injured himself.' I couldn't help but grimace at the thought. 'I'm sure I mentioned I'd baked the quiche at Arthur's when he was recovering. Jared and Richard crashed our lunch and ate most of it.'

Sheela nodded along. 'Yes, sounds about right for those boys... Whoa – hang on, hang on, hang on... You met *my* Richie through *your* Arthur?'

'Yes, that's what I just said – keep up!'

'Richard's childhood friend, little Arthur Fenwick, is this dreamboat you've been floating on for the past couple of weeks?'

'Well, uh – yes, I guess,' I said. 'You paint a vivid picture, Sheela.'

She chuckled. 'Thank you, my dear.'

'Your son "Richie" and Arthur's friend "Richard" are one and the same...'

'Why didn't you mention this earlier? We're practically related!'

'I'm only just now making the connection myself!' Exactly why I had my minor flip out a minute ago... No good revisiting that thought right now, I had my friend's son's wedding to get excited about for her. 'It'd never occurred to me, it's just *so* unlikely...'

'Yes... Richie's funny little friend, Arthur. A real worry wart that one. Haven't seen much of him since my Richie left home, I suppose he's grown up a bit – would never have imagined him as the love interest in anyone's story... Still, I should've made the connection!'

'There's been a fair bit of that going on lately. It's not like Arthur's a common name, how is this coming as a shock to everyone? Myself included.'

'Whoa,' Sheela said, holding a hand up to stop me. 'Just processing – obviously not my sharpest tonight, it seems – young Arthur Fenwick's gay?' She had her mouth open now, blinking at me in shock. After a moment she clamped her jaw shut, narrowed her eyes, and pursed her lips. She raised a finger in concentration, put it down, and back up again, processing the possibility… She nodded once with finality. 'Yep, checks out. Gay.'

'I can confirm,' I said with a smirk.

'Oh, I have no doubt you can,' Sheela said with a grin.

'Anyway, what are you doing here? Shouldn't you be busy organising things for the wedding or something?'

'Oh, no. Like I said, Lucy has it under control. I've given her my address book – very old fashioned, don't judge. I highlighted all the family guests – Richie wouldn't have a clue, after all. Colour-coded: green is a must invite; amber is only if there's space; and red is a definitely not, even if Richie suggests it.'

'For the best.'

'Yes, that boy doesn't appreciate the extended family politics.'

'A minefield, I'm sure.'

'That it is,' Sheela said, with pursed lips and wide eyes. 'And, there's been no time to send out save-the-dates, let alone the actual invites. Even I can recognise that the time for fancy invites in the post has long gone.'

'Surely nothing important gets sent by snail mail these days?'

'You'd be surprised! The bank just won't let it go, or the insurance company – I'd almost rather those got lost. But it's a pity that letters aren't a thing anymore, I do miss a nice stationery set.'

'I can't remember the last time I wrote more than the grocery list with a pen and paper.'

Sheela tutted. 'Anyway, the kids have been busy calling everyone. Again, I offered, but Lucy said she wouldn't have it, not after I'd already suggested I could do the hors d'oeuvres.'

'You're not?'

'I am.'

'You are,' I said, grinning. Now *this* was good news. 'With you in charge of the nibbles floating around, I don't think I'll have any space left for dinner.'

'Oh, stop it,' Sheela said, slapping me on the shoulder. 'My head is already quite big enough, thank you.'

'What are you thinking of doing, then?'

'It's a surprise!'

'Hah, so you don't know.'

'Nothing escapes you, Gabriel,' she said with a smile. 'I have a few ideas. Can't go too over-the-top – too many guests, and too little time to prepare. You'll have to wait and see, just like everyone else.'

'Fine! I'll start fasting now, make sure I have enough space in my stomach… Maybe after one more slice,' I said, snatching another piece of millionaire's shortbread.

Sheela laughed. 'So yes, other than that, I just have to organise myself and Iqbal. I dug out his suit – still fits, would you believe? – and sent it to the dry cleaners. Can't have him smelling musty, like the back of the wardrobe. And I found him a tie to match the dress I bought on the weekend,' she said, tapping me on the chest. 'Now, I don't mind admitting this to you, Gabriel, but I am going to look *stunning*. You know I'm a humble woman, but sometimes you've just got to admit it when you look bloody gorgeous. And I will.'

'I believe you.'

'I know it's all about what the mother of the bride will be wearing – and Lucy's mother is a very attractive lady – but stuff that. This mother of the groom won't be relegated to the back of the photo as some dowdy old matron.'

'Too right, Sheela,' I said. 'Those wedding photos are forever, and I have total faith you'll be shining in the front row.'

'Thank you,' she said, nodding in acknowledgement. 'You know I know my own thoughts well enough to not need reassurance, but it doesn't hurt either... And, of course, it's not a competition.'

'Of course not,' I said.

'But I won't be looking second best.'

'Not a chance.'

We nattered away the afternoon, checking in a steady flow of customers which now mostly comprised business people out for a hit before heading home for dinner.

'Is it that late already?' Sheela said.

'Shit! The floodlights.' I leapt from my seat and flicked them on at the switchboard. It wasn't getting dark yet, but the punters appreciated consistent lighting as we approached sunset.

'Oh yes, we can't be justifying Murray's micromanaging by forgetting, can we?'

The lights crackled and popped, coming on one by one as they warmed up – or whatever it was they were doing.

They were powerful beams – closer to what you see at stadiums than those hanging from your living room ceiling. They were still coming to life when I saw a coach pull into the parking area.

'That must be the big group Murray mentioned,' I said.

'I suppose we'd better do some actual work, then.'

# Chapter 5
# Where has the old boy brought us?

**ARTHUR**

I was starting to wonder how far Patty's detour was taking us when Desmond rose from his seat to talk to our driver. I couldn't hear what was said, but could tell by the jerk of Philip's head that he was surprised and uncertain. After another minute of Desmond in his ear, Philip slowly – reluctantly – nodded his head.

Shortly after that, the coach began to slow down.

Desmond turned around in the aisle to face everyone else. Silhouetted by the light coming through the windscreen, he appeared an ominous, looming figure. 'All right, folks,' he said in his booming voice. 'As agreed with the Garden Club, we've come to see these stately gardens.'

The coach was travelling at a crawl now.

'If you look out the port side' – a mischievous lightness to his tone now – 'you will notice our coach provides an unobstructed view over the manicured boundary hedges right into the gardens. I have instructed Mr Binfield to give us a gentle drive-by. So, please, soak it up – the flowers are looking lovely today. We will continue along this road, travelling the length of the gardens before we speed up again and move on to the day's first *proper* activity.'

I dared to turn and gauge Patty's reaction. Furious is what she was – so much so that she was lost for words. I held out little hope this would last.

Sure enough, a moment later she was out of her seat, this latest indignity piling onto her earlier repressed outrage. 'This is *not* what we agreed,' she said, blasting us all at full volume, 'and you know it!'

'I think you'll find, Mrs Binfield,' said Desmond, a picture of calm, 'that we agreed your members would "see" the gardens. There was no mention of stopping and ambling around or anything of the sort.'

Patty was spitting with rage. 'You know precisely what I meant! This is ridiculous!'

'Mrs Binfield, I don't think you realise, but the residents of the Sunset Villas retirement village are rather elderly – not as mobile as we once were. You saw the palaver getting everyone on the bus – that's half the day gone if we have to do that a few times back and forth. And these old bones can't be traipsing around vast grounds just to look at some shrubs. We've got some perfectly nice gardens back at the village.'

Patty was rendered speechless yet again.

'Oh!' Desmond said, ducking his head to peer out the window. 'That was the gardens. I hope everyone had a good look and took it all in. Mr Binfield, you can put your foot down again now, there's a good man.'

I was biting my cheek trying not to smile and Sam was snorting with amusement beside me. Since our first brief glance of the gardens, everyone had focused their attention to the battle of wills going on down the aisle.

Patty was screaming for the bus to be turned around, insisting that Philip was to park at the visitor's centre and let everyone off. And Desmond responded to every hurled demand, instruction, and threat by pointing out that there wasn't the time. Meanwhile, Philip attempted to sink further and further into his seat while maintaining control of the coach. Patty's friend watched on, equal parts mortified and delighted.

After minutes of this heated exchange, in which we'd only gone further from the gardens, Patty realised it was a lost cause. Everyone eased back into their seats when they saw the show was over. But where before there had been a general overlapping of excited conversations, now there was only silence.

Patty had been in her seat for a mere moment before she leapt up again, this time heading for the rear of the coach. She snatched Nora's sherry, filled her travel mug and returned to her seat.

A short while later, the woman next to Patty – uncomfortable in the silence and too pumped from all the excitement to sit still – leant across to introduce herself.

'You must be Patty's neighbour, Arthur?' she said, smiling past Patty's furious expression. 'I'm Sharon. Sharon Sheffield.'

It hit me – I knew how I knew this woman now.

'It's pronounced Sha-RON – important distinction – emphasis on the second syllable, you see?'

Gabriel's landlady, who had seen me half-naked on the

way to his bedroom only a few days ago.

'The rose of Sharon,' I said, repeating what Gabriel had recounted to me. 'The lily of the valley.'

'Oh, yes! How delightful, you know the story of my name's origin?'

I said that I did indeed, but didn't mention Gabriel's hilarious and exaggerated version.

Sharon told me the origin story all over again, just to be sure. I nodded along, only glad that she still hadn't recognised me.

'Here we are!' Desmond said, cutting off Sharon's epic tale.

I took the opportunity to turn away, looking out the window to see a weather-beaten, barely legible sign as we pulled into a driveway.

'"Roger's Range",' Sam said, eyes wide with surprise. 'Doesn't look like the kind of place I'd expected we'd be going today.'

\*\*\*

I took in the gravel parking area with Sam as Mr Binfield helped the residents down the stairs. It was an ordeal, getting off taking even longer than getting on – I can understand why Desmond wanted to do away with any unnecessary stops.

Sam nudged me and nodded towards the only other vehicle in the parking area – a rusty old truck with mismatched panels which appeared to be held together solely by obscene political bumper stickers. 'Tow bar,' she said with a smirk.

I did a double table – surely not? 'Is that—'

'Sure is,' she said, chuckling. 'A hefty set of testicles.'

'Well, shit...' I said. 'I mean, a brass ball bag hanging from your tow bar... what the fuck?'

'Where has the old boy brought us?'

Where, indeed? I caught the reactions to our destination as everyone disembarked, most portraying variations on incredulity.

Patty, Sharon, and a few of the other Garden Club members were not subtle in screwing up their faces in disgust. However, many of the elderly residents were intrigued, looking around with curiosity. My friends Gladys, Gerry, Nora, and Charles fitted in this camp too. Maud was her usual floaty, oblivious self.

Then there was Mrs Abbington. I saw her halt at the top of the coach steps, looking out, aghast at the state of this place. Poor dear Elspeth was well out of her comfort zone today. I could see her warring within herself about whether she should return to her seat in protest and wait it out until it was time to return to the Sunset Villas. Her face set with determination, I saw her decide it wouldn't do to cause a fuss – no one could accuse her of not being a gracious guest. This all occurred in a matter of seconds before she descended to the dusty ground.

'Oh! There he is,' Sam said, 'Roger himself.'

A wiry old man emerged from amongst a ramshackle smattering of corrugated iron sheds and a fenced pigsty, lit cigarette dangling from the corner of his mouth. He was kitted out head-to-toe in camouflage duds. Pitched over at the waist, he shuffled towards the growing cluster of elderly residents – many of whom were probably his junior.

He arrived as the last of the passengers disembarked and clapped a hand on his own chest. 'Roger,' he said by way of introduction, his voice deep, raspy, and gruff, that of the lifelong smoker. He stared at us all for a moment through a puff of smoke, then jerked his head back. 'You're late, let's get on with it.'

Without another word, Roger turned and led us back the way he'd come. Despite the obvious effort, he maintained a good pace that the residents struggled to keep up with.

The place was a mess – dilapidated buildings, half-collapsed fences, rusted out pieces of machinery lying around. Now, to say Roger's setup was a pigsty would be doing the pigs a disservice – their enclosure was probably the tidiest aspect of the place.

While we picked our way through the yard, trying to avoid snagging our clothes on stray barbed wire, I caught Elspeth whispering in Maud's ear. Maud reached into her handbag before handing something off to Elspeth, who then made a beeline for Nora. She snatched the bottle of sherry – how had that not been finished yet? – turned aside, threw back what must have been a fistful of Maud's anxiety pills, and downed them with a slug straight from the bottle.

'Did you see that?' Sam said, smirking at Elspeth's shady behaviour. 'Granny drug dealers.'

'This is very much not her scene,' I said. 'Looks like she needs a little help to get through the day.'

We passed through the post-apocalyptic wasteland of tin shacks before Roger led us out onto a vast, freshly mown lawn overlooking a lush, vegetated valley. The contrast to what we'd just walked through was shocking – this was where Roger focused his energies.

The steep slopes were carpeted in thick greenery, giving way to pastures dotted with occasional cattle on the more gently sloping land further down the valley.

A chorus of oohs and aahs greeted the scene as the group shuffled to a standstill, taking in the fresh air with the vista. Even the Garden Club members were in awe of the landscape, breathing deeply in appreciation. And not a car engine, siren, or any other sound of the city to be heard – just the birds and the insects bringing life to this bucolic setting.

The peaceful appreciation was shattered moments later by a bang, causing a few of the residents to lose their footing in shock. I caught one, holding him steady until he'd composed himself, then I scanned for the source of the noise.

A few paces away stood Roger, still pitched over at the waist, but now with a shotgun cracked in half held across his chest. I'd been so taken by the view of the gully that I hadn't noticed the row of targets behind Roger, set off to the side at the end of the lawn, with trees lining the hill in behind – to catch any stray bullets, I presumed.

'Bah. Ignore those,' Roger said, dismissing the targets with his free hand as he followed my gaze. 'For the kids. Too easy to hit something standing still. No good. Today, we're clay bird shooting – or clay pigeon shooting – whatever you want to call it. Nothing on hunting live game, mind. Still, it's better than them targets there. Let's get cracking.' At least that's what I think he said – his gravelly rumble of a voice meant I couldn't be sure.

He led us over to a contraption which looked like the bastard offspring of a wheelbarrow and a push lawnmower, with a set of rails sticking out the top stacked with bright orange discs. 'This puts the birds up,' Roger said, nudging the apparatus with his boot. 'And this takes them down,' he added, patting the gun in his grasp. 'That's it.'

He rattled off a string of half-formed sentences – I managed to catch something about 'down-the-line' and 'trap' and 'follow through', but I couldn't stitch much of it into any semblance of sense. I figured he was calling the gun an 'over and under', with the two barrels stacked one atop the other. But if we weren't careful, I thought the day might end up closer to 'over and out' with this elderly crowd.

One thing he did make clear, however, was that the gun should only ever be pointed in the direction of the hillside behind the stationary targets, no matter if it was loaded or not, no matter if the safety was on or not. Sensible advice, I thought.

'Lad' – Roger waved me over towards his contraption – 'you're in charge of the trap while I sort these oldies out, you hear?'

'Uh—'

'Good. See this?' He nudged a pad on the grass which had a wire trailing out and connected to the 'trap'. It looked like the foot pedal on Nana's sewing machine. 'Hoof that, will you?'

'What's it do?'

'Just do as you're told, boy. Haven't got all day, have we?'

I wasn't about to argue with the man holding the gun. I stepped on the pedal and the trap sprung into life with an arm flinging one of the orange discs straight out into the air, hurling it in the direction of the lush hillside with the targets at the base.

With a swift turn, Roger pulled his gun up and fired. The bang – coming from only a single pace away – was deafening, and even though I knew it was coming this time, it still gave me a fright. I had a moment to recover before

66

Roger fired another shot – his second and final. The orange clay bird sailed on, only breaking apart when it hit the meticulously trimmed lawn.

'Fuckfuckfuckfuck,' Roger swore under his breath, grabbing shells out of his pocket to reload. 'Pull!'

'What?'

'Again!' Roger said. 'Step on the bloody pedal.'

'Right.' I stomped on the pedal to fire another clay bird.

Roger fired again, hitting the clay bird on the first shot. It shattered into pieces, the shards raining down on the lawn. 'Better,' he said, cracking the gun in half and nodding to himself as he turned. 'Right, who's first?'

I could see he was confronted with a wall of apprehensive faces. But not Maud – she'd flung her handbag into Elspeth's arms and shot forwards. 'Oh, yes,' she said. 'I think I'll have a turn.'

That was unexpected, but Desmond looked pleased that someone other than himself was willing to give it a go.

Roger muttered away to Maud, adjusting her stance and making sure she held the butt of the gun right into her shoulder. 'Or you'll put it all out of joint, can't have that.' Maud giggled, enjoying being made a fuss of. I just hoped she was paying attention.

'Right,' Roger said, stepping back. 'Just say the word.'

Maud turned to face us. 'What was the—'

'Face forwards, my dear.'

'Oh, yes,' Maud said before pointing the gun back away from us. 'Yes, apologies.'

'Say "pull" when you're ready.'

'Of course, of course.' Maud nodded to herself, repositioned the butt of the gun properly in her shoulder. 'Pull!'

I stomped on the pedal, releasing the clay bird. Maud followed the trajectory and fired. The clay bird sailed on, and she fired again – it exploded into a shower of shards.

Maud hooted with delight and spun around to—

'Forwards!'

'Oh, yes!' Maud finished the spin to face back down the line. Roger shuffled over and cracked the gun.

'Safe,' he said, and patted Maud on the arm. 'Well done, young lady.'

Maud was glowing with pride as she rejoined the group to many congratulations.

With Maud's early success, the residents and club members were falling over each other to have their turn. Roger left me in charge of restocking the trap when the supply of clay birds in the 'magazine' ran low and launching the trap whenever I heard a 'pull!'

'Who knew this lot had such bloodlust,' I said as Sam approached.

'It will certainly get the blood pumping,' she said. 'We'd better keep an eye on the coach's back seat, make sure these folks don't get too frisky on the drive back home – victors returning from battle, desperate to satisfy their thirst.'

'Ew. That's – that's gross. I don't want to think about that.'

'Why not? Don't you think the oldies deserve a bit of hanky panky, too?' She smiled at me.

'Sure, I guess,' I said. 'Just not in the back seat of the coach.'

'I'm sure you wouldn't mind a roll around the back seat if you were all fired up and there was an eligible bachelor kicking around here somewhere…'

My imagination couldn't help itself: my thoughts went

straight to Gabriel – who else? Sam was right, of course. I couldn't think of many – or any? – other things I'd rather be doing.

'Arthur?' Sam said.

'Hmm?' I said, coming down from my daydream.

'They're waiting for—'

'I'm ready! Can't hold this thing up much longer,' an insistent Nora said, poised with the gun, ready to fire. 'Hurry up and pull!'

I stomped on the pedal to fire the clay bird.

'Where'd you go, Arthur?' Sam said, her mouth quirked in a smile. 'Thinking of pulling on something else – or someone else – were you?'

***

The clay bird shooting was a runaway success. After everyone had overcome the initial shock, and Gladys suggested the oldies turned their hearing aids off, they were all excited to give it a go. Some even knocked a few clay birds out of the sky.

The elderly hunters were ravenous. Trestle tables set up on the lawn were laden with club sandwiches cut into little triangles – courtesy of the Sunset Villas kitchens – along with fresh pots of tea.

With the intermittent bang of the shotgun gone, you could really appreciate the idyllic landscape again. Everyone was chatting amiably, sipping their tea and munching away. The sandwiches were delicious: juicy tomato, fresh lettuce, cheddar, mayonnaise, crisp rashers of bacon and slices of ham, all sandwiched between two slices of white bread.

The perfect picnic lunch with a stunning outlook – as long as you oriented yourself towards the beautiful vista and didn't turn around to face Roger's bombsite of a yard and the pigsty—

I paused mid-chew and turned around. Pink snouts snuffled through the railings, with occasional grunts as the pigs lumbered around their enclosure. I swallowed my mouthful as I looked down guiltily at the last bite of my sandwich – I couldn't do it. It was silly – having already devoured the flesh of their fellows – but it felt sadistic to keep munching on ham and bacon in front of them.

I kept my guilty carnivorous thoughts to myself as I sneaked the last mouthful into the bin and finished my tea before Desmond rounded up everyone again, shepherding us back to the coach to begin the lengthy embarkation process.

***

'Aren't you two getting on well, then?' Patty said when she'd taken her seat, turning to her friend for confirmation.

'Yes, they are quite an attractive pair,' Sharon said, pleased to be involved in this matchmaking scheme.

'They are, aren't they?' Patty said, beaming as she leant across the aisle to get a better look at us. 'Yes, I knew it.'

'It's all for nothing, Aunty Pat,' Sam said, feigning regret. 'He's given his heart to another!'

Way to pile on the melodrama. 'I—'

'Oh no, is that right, Arthur?' Patty said. 'You've never said anything.'

'We haven't been seeing each other long…' I said. 'But you've already met, actually.' Here goes—

'I've never seen you with a girl at the house.'

'Uh, I'm not seeing a girl… I'm seeing a guy. His name's Gabriel, he tripped in the hallway when you stopped over the other morning.'

'Oh, the one in a hurry for the bathroom?'

'Yes.'

'After leaving your bedroom…' she said, almost to herself.

'Yes.'

'Wearing only his underpants…'

'Yes.'

'Nothing else to cover that body…'

'Yes.'

'First thing in the morning…'

'Yes.'

'Meaning he'd stayed over…'

'Yes.'

'And…' Patty went scarlet, realisation dawning, finally. She leant back into her seat, staring straight ahead at the headrest in front, not saying another word.

'I—'

'Give her a minute,' Sam said, stopping me from saying any more. 'You caught her on the hop. She's just recalibrating.'

'Might have overdone it,' I said quietly.

'Well, I don't know how you could've said any less,' Sam said. 'A minimum is required to get the point across.'

'True, so awkward though…' And we were stuck on a coach together, within arm's reach of each other but avoiding eye contact.

'Did I hear you say this guy's name was Gabriel?' Sam said.

'Yeah,' I said, smiling. I knew it was gushy, but I couldn't help the warm rush of feelings at just hearing someone else saying his name, despite my current extreme discomfort.

'I am *so* stupid...' Sam said slowly before bursting out laughing.

'What? Why?'

I was still trying to get an explanation out of Sam, who was crying with laughter now, unable to utter a word, when Desmond tapped me on the shoulder.

'Not the most composed girl, is she, Mrs Binfield's niece? Give her one of these – my granddaughter made them, sweet girl – they'll calm her down.' Desmond held up a familiar tin – the one he'd won last night – but the sad biscuit selection had been turfed out, and in their place... 'Afternoon tea: my *special* brownie. Does wonders for my aches and pains, and will be good after the kickback from that gun. Soothing for the soul, too. You kids had better grab one now – they might not last another round. Our Elspeth was particularly taken with them.'

He nudged the tin at me and I took one each for myself and Sam. I gave it a sniff before taking a bite – one guess what the 'special' ingredient was.

'And that port Charles won last night shouldn't be far behind – help you wash down the brownie. But don't muck around, we're approaching our next activity – I'm sure you'll enjoy it.' He gave me a dirty wink. 'Nora asked me to add this to the schedule after bingo last night. Called them up first thing this morning. The grump on the other end of the line huffed and puffed about us being such a big group, and calling so last minute, but he fitted us in. He's charging us an arm and a leg – you'd think he'd be pleased to make so much money, all in one hit.'

Desmond left, shaking his head as he continued up the coach. As predicted, the port soon followed. I poured some for Sam, whose giggling fit had now subsided into the occasional chuckle, then passed the port over to Patty without looking, and she took the bottle without a word.

I turned to face Sam. 'So—'

'I was at the pub with Gabriel last night,' she said, still chuckling. 'And I've *just* made the connection – *such* an idiot – that you're the Arthur he was talking about, the one he's going to the wedding with, one of Richard Singh's Best Men.'

'How do you know—'

'I'm one of Lucy's best friends!'

'You're bloody not…'

'I bloody well am. We met at work.'

'What's Gabriel going to say about this?' I said, shaking my head. All these connections – so improbable, what a farce!

'Looks like we'll be seeing more of each other this week, after all.'

'Pity we couldn't have taken each other to the wedding,' Sam said. 'What a pair we'd make.'

'Patty would've loved—'

'Just think what we could've got up to *after* the wedding.'

'Ah—'

'You and Gabriel though – that's hot,' she said with a wink. 'Just running that imagery through my rather vivid imagination…'

'You wh—'

'Ladies and gentlemen,' Desmond said from the front of

the coach, cutting off my protest. 'We have arrived.'

I glanced out the coach window as we pulled into a parking area, saw the vast mesh fence looming above with floodlights coming on behind the massive sign which read: Topdrive Golf.

# Chapter 6
# He is a handsome lad, isn't he?

**GABRIEL**

'Have you ever seen anything like it?' Sheela said.

'It's just… so slow,' I said.

'Painful to watch.'

'Is that a walking frame?' I couldn't quite tell – the powerful floodlights were focused on the range, not the parking area.

'And someone swigging a bottle of booze?'

'What a crew,' I said. 'Let's go see if they need a hand.'

Sheela and I approached the gathering mass. Murray would've lost it if he knew – 'There must be at least one staff member at the reception desk at all times' – but these were the only people coming or going. And what an odd bunch – this was not to be missed.

As they disembarked, it brought with them wafts of—

'Is that gunpowder I smell?' Sheela said.

'Yes! That's it.' I hadn't been able to place it immediately myself because it was so unexpected. 'And something else? Smells more like a university campus than a coach full of pensioners.'

'Oh, hello young-man-in-uniform.' An elderly woman had peeled away from the group to approach us. She had a glint of mischief in her eye as she proffered a biscuit tin decorated with pastoral scenes. 'Would you like a brownie' – she paused to check my name badge – 'Gabriel?' She seemed to repeat my name to herself a few times under her breath, flashes of almost recognition and confusion playing across her expressive face. She shook her head and continued, 'Our friend's granddaughter baked them. Does wonders for my aches and pains. *Most* relaxing.'

'Well, that answers that,' Sheela said, unable to contain herself by this point.

'I'd better not,' I said to the older woman with the biscuit tin. 'Can't be too "relaxed" while I'm working – have to keep an eye on you troublemakers, don't I?'

The older woman was delighted, laughing and touching my arm. 'Oh my dear boy, you are charming. And I am the biggest troublemaker of them all, so you had best keep a very close eye on me,' she said with a wink. 'My name's Nora Appleby, by the way. I keep a room at Sunset Villas, and you're most welcome to visit any time, day or night.' She smiled and rejoined the group, offering some more of her pot brownie to the other oldies.

'Did she—'

'Yes,' Sheela said with her widest grin yet. 'A stoned 80-something-year-old woman invited you back to her room.'

I couldn't help but smile. Then, as I was about to lead this apparently gun-toting, weed-munching, straight-from-the-bottle-swigging crew towards the driving range, I heard a shrill call from the coach.

'Mr Bedford! Here you are, at the driving range, as promised.'

'Mrs Sheffield, this is a surprise,' I said, as she bustled over, not willing to comment on the pleasantness of the surprise. I did want to ask where *else* she expected me to be, but at the same time I didn't want to know…

'Earning your rent, I see.' My landlady chuckled in a way that was just asking for a quick, sharp jab to the privilege. 'Such a responsible young man.' Said with pride, as if she'd had a hand in my upbringing. She'd directed that boastful yet condescending comment at Sheela who stood beside me, no doubt expecting to find in her a like-minded soul.

'Mrs Sheffield, this is my colleague and good friend Sheela Singh,' I said.

'Hello, my name is Sharon.' Emphasis on the second syllable, as we all bloody well knew. 'And how many times must I remind you, dear boy? You're part of my tenant family – we mustn't be so formal. It's Sharon, not Mrs Sheffield.' Yet she still insisted on referring to me by my surname – I just didn't understand. Sharon turned to Sheela and said, 'I was starting to wonder if young Mr Bedford really worked here, thought maybe it was just an excuse to rush off whenever I called him over for a little chat.'

'I couldn't imagine why he'd want to escape.' Sheela's tone was frosty – no doubt the result of my frequent gripes about my landlady. Perhaps my friend felt the need to defend me here? That was nice.

'It's just that he works so hard,' Sharon said, shaking her head. 'He always seems to be coming here for a shift, always making more money. Young people should be focusing on their studies.'

'You must be charging him too much rent, then,' Sheela said.

Sharon was taken aback, unable to respond for a moment, before offering an awkward chuckle and shifting away.

'This is going to be an entertaining evening,' I said to Sheela with a smile.

'That's one word for it.'

'Thank you for that, by the way.'

'Anything for you, sweetheart,' she said, patting me on the arm. 'Now, let's get this lot through. Looks like they'll be unloading for a while longer, and if they take anywhere near this long to get on the range, we'll be here all night.'

\*\*\*

Sheela left me on the front desk to check everyone in – she hated the paperwork, though that's not how she pitched it. Her argument was that she needed to be out on the range because she was older – could better appreciate the pitfalls of a 'more mature set of bones' and could direct the players accordingly. She took them through stretches, positioned them at the tee, and instructed them on how to hit the golf balls.

Compared to this lot, though, Sheela was a spring chicken. The group primarily comprised septuagenarians and octogenarians, with the occasional nonagenarian, too – men and women – as well as a bunch of women closer in age to Sheela, including my landlady of all people.

You may wonder how I knew their ages? Well, this was

because I was helping each player sign their lives away on Murray's waivers. If I thought the bus unloading dragged on, this was next level.

I got a few of them going at the same time, lined up along my reception desk with pen and paper. Half of them chuckled and giggled their way through, turning the 'Health' section into a game, ticking each applicable box with a flourish – I heard a few calls of 'Royal flush!' or 'Bingo!' They'd obviously partaken in the roadie refreshments to be so delighted by listing their various ailments.

The other half of my form-fillers either muttered about political correctness gone mad, commented on how ridiculous this all was, or expressed bafflement at what a driving range could possibly need to know *that* for. There were no victory calls from this lot, only tuts and head shaking. One such person was a middle-aged woman I realised I recognised. It was Arthur's nosy neighbour, and her face went white the second she saw me before turning away hurriedly to complete her form in private.

Murray had insisted we get each new player to sign a waiver form before handing over clubs and ball baskets, and he'd have my head if I didn't leave a stack of completed forms for him to trawl through tomorrow. He'd been particularly insistent on this since Arthur caned himself. Murray's argument was that Arthur was a young, healthy, fit guy – you'll hear no arguments from me there – and if he could injure himself, then this coach full of geriatrics were guaranteed to throw something out.

Not only was I answering a constant stream of relevant queries from those completing the paperwork, but also fielding questions about what it was like working here, my studies, what I thought about the weather on the weekend, whether I had a girlfriend, whether I thought the level of investment in transport infrastructure was sufficient, my family, what I had for lunch – anything and everything. It was quite the grilling, but I think they were just keeping themselves amused. Some questions I deflected and others I was happy to answer – either way it filled the time. My elderly mob had soon passed through, leaving only a young couple waiting patiently off to the side, just round the corner.

'One moment,' I said, gathering up the last of the forms before I could check them in. 'Sorry to hold you up, big group to—'

While rambling my pleasantries, I looked up properly for the first time to see a face framed with loose red curls and sporting a delighted grin. 'Sam!' I said, eyes shooting wide. 'What are you doing here?'

'Hello, my sweet,' Sam said. 'Look who I brought with me.'

She tugged at her companion's shirt, dragging him around the corner and into view.

'Arthur!' I said, leaping to my feet, my chair clattering to the ground behind me.

He looked shy – uncomfortably, embarrassingly, adorably shy.

'Hi,' he said.

'Hi,' I said, too busy processing what he was doing here to come up with anything else. Never mind that he knew Sam – I'd have to ask about that one later. I realised now that the mob of oldies I'd just pushed through must be the bingo friends Arthur inherited from his Nana. And today was the big mystery outing Arthur had mentioned.

We were both still standing motionless on opposite sides of the desk.

'You look like a pair of jumpy maidens,' Sam said, yanking us both out of the moment. 'So modest... I thought you two were banging?'

If I thought Arthur was bashful before, this comment really ramped it up with his eyes going wide and a flash of colour clawing up his neck.

Only for a moment, though. His face morphed into a look of determination, then without any more time for thought he stepped forwards, leant in and planted a brief kiss on my lips.

'Sam,' he said as he stepped back, in a tone that suggested he was delivering a terminal diagnosis, not a friendly introduction. 'This is my boyfriend, Gabriel.'

I felt a flush of heat myself, and I wasn't able to tear my eyes off him – I was so proud. It was only us three. And based on the little time I'd spent with Sam, she was the kind of person who could lift the mood in any situation, put people at ease. But still, introducing your same-sex date to someone – anyone – especially when you're fresh out of the closet – that takes grit.

'And, uh...' Arthur said, 'it looks like you've already met...' He trailed off, his timidity reasserting itself – his declaration apparently having spent his reserves of boldness.

Sam had her lips between her teeth, biting down on a grin that was desperate to escape, as she swept forward to give me a big, tight hug.

She stepped back, narrowed her eyes and lifted her index finger to her lips. 'Yes,' she said. 'Yes, I think you'll do just fine for my Arthur.'

'*Your* Arthur?' I said.

'Of course,' Sam said, arm around Arthur's shoulders now. 'I mean, we only met this morning, but I feel like I've known him forever. We've practically been betrothed for months – even a year, perhaps? – as far as Aunty Pat is concerned.'

She turned to squeeze Arthur's cheeks. 'And we would've made such gorgeous babies. Alas! Not to be – Arthur's not interested in my foofoo or tatas, are you my sweet? He's all about what this angelic man before us has to offer.' She was back to squeezing Arthur into a side hug and now sweeping her free arm to gesture up and down my person. 'Don't blame you, to be honest. I would certainly not say no to a ride on—'

'OK!' I said, not wanting to hear any further details, which I am sure she'd be quite willing to provide.

'Fine, yes, OK.' Sam held up her hands in surrender. 'I'll leave that to you two.' She waggled her eyebrows like a filthy lecher.

'Uh, thanks, I guess?' I caught Arthur's eye. He seemed undecided, not sure if he was outraged at his boyfriend being objectified, shy about his sex life being discussed, or delighted that he had a sex life in the first place.

'I can just watch,' Sam said, 'maybe give you boys a hand if you—'

'Nope. Not a chance.' That would not be happening.

'Fine,' Sam said, making a show of being put out. 'I'll keep my hands to myself, just watch from the corner.'

'Sam,' I said, playing along with the charade. 'You are an attractive and uh – and persistent woman. And I haven't discussed this with Arthur, but I'm making the call: this will not be happening.'

82

Sam sighed theatrically, then smiled. 'A girl can dream… But I wouldn't dare get between you boys – that'd just get awkward. And there's no way I'd be third-wheeling it for anyone – my ego couldn't handle it. You can send me the sex tape afterwards, that's fine.'

Arthur laughed and Sam smiled in response. He seemed much more relaxed now, and I was in awe of her masterful defusion of Arthur's earlier apprehension.

Arthur came around my side of the desk to perch on Sheela's chair, and the three of us soon relaxed into easy conversation about the driving range and the highlights from today's big outing.

***

I was chatting away with Arthur and Sam, wondering if Sheela might need a hand on the front line, when a gaggle of purposeful pensioners made their way back from their bay.

My first thought was that they appeared to be as mobile as when they'd arrived – no hands clutching lower backs, no hobbled gaits – success!

My shameless admirer – Nora, I believe – led the pack, followed by a gruff-looking old boy, a stereotypically cosy-looking grandmother, and a finely dressed gentleman wielding the most impressive moustache I think I've ever encountered. When they'd emerged from the coach, I thought they were a random group of pensioners out for a swing, but with Sam and Arthur following up at the tail-end I now knew these people for who they were: Arthur's Nana's friends. Friends he'd adopted as his own – literally a village of stand-in grandparents. The way he spoke about them, I understood how important they were to him. But as far as I was aware, he still hadn't told them about his sexuality, and I had to wonder if I was important enough for him to commit to coming out.

I glanced at Arthur to see he wore that same determined face he'd had earlier.

'Nora, Gerry, Gladys, and Charles,' Arthur said, gesturing stiffly to each in turn. 'I want to introduce you to Gabriel.'

'Yes, yes. Thank you, dear,' Nora said, waving Arthur away. 'We are quite capable of reading a name badge for ourselves.' She turned to me and smiled. 'Hello again, Gabriel. This handsome young man and I have already met. I have high hopes that we may become even better acquainted later... That is, unless you've had a change of heart, my dear Arthur?'

OK, perhaps that one didn't see herself standing in for the grandmother role...

A bark of laughter burst from Sam. She copped a shady glance from Nora for her insolence, but then the older woman dismissed it quickly – she was on a mission. 'I've just now realised... With a name like "Gabriel" that must cause some confusion.'

'Uh... why's that?'

'Working with someone with such a similar-sounding name, of course!' Nora said, as if speaking to a simpleton. 'I had an Isadora in my class at school one year, terribly confusing.'

I didn't get a chance to ask what she was on about as the big, bear-like old man, Gerry, cut in. 'That's by the by, Nora.' He turned back to me. 'Our Arthur's too shy to bring the subject of his affections to meet us, you see, so we have done the legwork for him in coming here. It's clear to us at bingo – those who haven't gone completely blind, anyway – that he's all tied up in knots, head over heels.'

'We've taken it upon ourselves as honorary grandparents,' said Charles, the prodigious moustache-owner, gesturing to those in his merry band, 'to come and make our introductions.'

'Yes! We've come to meet my love-rival,' Nora said. 'I have to know what I'm up against. I asked our Desmond – a rascal, but still useful on occasion – to add the driving range to today's agenda after Arthur mentioned it last night. It was all very last minute, but Dez was just as curious about the one who's set our Arthur's heart aflutter. And so, here we are.'

Arthur was mortified, his jaw working itself open and closed, unable to come up with anything. I desperately wanted to step in and help him out, but this was his show and he needed to be the one to draw back the curtains.

Sam was enthralled, and looked on the verge of bursting – barely keeping a lid on her delight lest she miss a second of the performance.

Arthur still hadn't managed to form words before Gladys, the grandmotherly one, stepped in. 'It is quite clear to us that young Arthur has found his special someone.' Gladys paused to look around her fellow pensioners, receiving a nod from each. 'And, it saddens me, but it is as they say: we're not getting any younger.' She rested her hand on Arthur's. 'I'm sure if our friend, your Nana, was still here, she would have loved to meet this sweetheart of yours.'

What a power play. And it appeared to have hit its mark – Arthur's eyes glistened more than usual.

'So,' Nora said after leaving a few moments to let that sink in, looking between Arthur and myself, 'where can we find this Gabrielle?'

'*What?*' Arthur said, utter bewilderment apparently the only thing that could extract words from his frozen self.

Sam finally exploded, buckled over with hands on knees, laughing without restraint.

Now it was the oldies' turn to look confused – concerned eyes darting between me, Arthur, and Sam.

Arthur took a deep breath and cleared his throat. Sam got herself together, holding back a smirk as she gave Arthur a quick thumbs-up.

'Nora, Charles, Gerry, Gladys… Desmond misheard – there is no *Gabrielle* working at the driving range.' He stood up, stepped to my side and put an arm around my shoulder. 'This is *Gabriel*, my *boyfriend*… I'm gay.'

He stood fast, maintaining contact. I put my arm across my chest, resting my hand on his – a show of gratitude and support.

You could see the clockwork gears grinding behind their eyes, then, ever so slowly, the light of understanding.

'But… are you sure, though?' Gladys said.

'Not just a phase?' That was Nora, still holding out hope.

'What about that nice girl – was it Jenny? Penny? Whichever, the one you took to your school ball?' Gerry said.

'No, not a phase. And Jenny was just a friend,' Arthur said, clearly a little peeved that they were talking about some girl from school.

'Yes, she wasn't clever enough for our Arthur,' Gladys said.

Nora sighed, then after a moment nodded and

scrunched up her face. 'And she had that awful laugh.'

'More like a cackle, you remember?' Gladys said.

'Like some evil witch stirring her cauldron,' Nora said, smiling while she did the action and attempted the cackle.

'Pretty little thing, though,' Charles said.

'Looks aren't everything, Charles,' Gerry said. 'Need something between the ears, too.'

'True,' Charles said, conceding the point easily. 'And young Gabriel seems like he's got his head screwed on. He is a handsome lad too, isn't he?'

'You mustn't judge a book by its cover,' Gladys said in her no-nonsense voice.

'But that is precisely what people do, is that not the case?' Charles countered. 'You can't honestly say that you don't.'

'Well... perhaps, but we all know it's what's on the inside that counts.'

'An unappealing book isn't going to catch your eye, is it?' Charles was obviously not going to let this one slide.

'Well, no.'

'You're not going to think, "My, what a dreary-looking book, I must pick it up." So, you'll never know what's on the inside, whether it's any good or not.' Charles made a solid point.

Gladys wasn't ready to let this go either. 'People aren't books—'

'Neither do all of us have the time or the energy to *sample* every book on offer...' Charles trailed off while looking pointedly at Nora.

Nora looked affronted. 'I do no such—'

'What I'm trying to say,' Charles said, holding his hands up in surrender. 'What I'm trying to say is this: our Arthur obviously liked the look of this particular book,' he said, gesturing to me. 'Gabriel caught his eye, so he grabbed him off the shelf, opened him up' – did this guy hear himself? – 'and he must have liked what he found inside because now he's telling people this is his *favourite book*.'

There was a short pause while everyone considered this thought.

'I think we've strayed from the matter at hand,' Gerry said.

'What's that?' said another of the old boys who'd returned from the tees. 'What's everyone doing back here, anyway?'

'Desmond, our Arthur's gay,' Gladys said.

'Arthur's gay?' Desmond said. 'Happy gay, or soap-drop-in-the-shower gay?'

'Both, I expect. That's his boyfriend, Gabriel,' Charles said. 'Handsome *and* clever, as we have established.'

'Is that right?' Desmond said, looking at me before turning to Arthur. 'Why didn't you say so?'

'I uh – I just did.'

'So you have,' he said, smiling as he clapped Arthur on the back. 'Hah! Didn't realise our boy batted for the other team.'

'You can't say that!' Gladys said.

'Why not?'

'It's offensive.'

'Is not,' Desmond said. 'If I wanted to be offensive, I'm sure I could come up with—'

'It is,' Gladys insisted. 'The gays don't like sports, so it's offensive to compare them to cricket players.'

'Now *that* is offensive! To suggest gays can't play sports,' Desmond said, clearly pleased with himself. I suspected he might be the type usually getting called out, so he was taking delight in being on the high road.

'Merely presumptuous,' Charles said.

'Gabriel, do you like sports?' Gladys said.

'Don't answer that!' Desmond had his hand up to stop me saying a word.

'Get an eye-full of that specimen: those shoulders, that chest, those legs!' Nora said. 'You don't get a body like that sitting around all day.'

My head had been whipping back and forth following the bickering oldies, but now all eyes were on me and I didn't know where to look.

'And he works at a golf driving range – golf is a sport,' Gerry said.

'Debatable,' Charles said.

'Don't get me started. But while we're on the topic, shall we discuss chess?'

'Don't you bring chess into this.' This sounded like well-trodden ground.

'So, who's the king and who's the queen?' Gladys said in a misguided attempt to bring the conversation back in line.

Arthur choked. Sam continued to watch on in fascination.

'What *are* you talking about, Gladys?' Desmond said.

'Well, uh… Who's the man and who's the woman? You know…' Gladys flailed, too coy to say or demonstrate what she really meant.

'They're both men – that's the whole point.' Nora eyed us appreciatively. 'Mm, just look at them.'

'Precisely. And if we're still comparing them to chess pieces – I think they're both knights,' Charles said.

'Certainly not bishops,' Gerry said with a chuckle.

'Amen to that.'

'But… *where* does it go?' That Gladys sure was persistent.

'Where does *what* go?' Nora said, with an innocent smile on her face now. She knew precisely what the other woman was saying, but delighted in her discomfort.

'You know… the, uh—'

'It goes wherever they please, I assume,' Gerry said, rescuing Gladys from having to spell it out, much to Nora's displeasure.

'But – and – but there's two… you know. So, whose do they use?'

'Both, I expect.' Nora was practically drooling now.

'I thought we'd already established this,' Charles said. 'Both being men and all.'

'We have,' Gerry said, giving Gladys a stern look.

'I just wanted to be sure.' You could see she was determined to understand, but wasn't quite there yet.

'Gladys has much to ponder,' Gerry said.

'I know I will be giving this some serious thought later tonight,' Nora said, looking at me and Arthur expectantly. 'But for now, why don't we ask the boys?'

The others turned to look too. They wouldn't ask, but you could tell they were dying to know.

'I love you all dearly,' Arthur said, crossing his arms over his chest. 'But that's none of your bloody business.'

'Hear, hear,' Charles said as Gerry slammed a palm on the table and laughed.

'Arthur, dear,' Nora said after everyone had settled down again. 'You know how my door is always open for you?'

'Yes, I am well aware, thank you Nora,' he said. 'But, as

you can see, I have a boyfriend.'

'Of course, of course. And I have extended the invite to Gabriel, too,' she said. 'Though, this was before I realised you two were an item.'

'Uh huh...'

'I realised I've been going about this all wrong, trying to woo you away from your mystery lover, though I can't understand what your excuse was before—'

'You're not his type,' Gerry said.

'No, I don't believe that is so, Gerry,' Nora said, unwilling to accept that she could not draw the eye of any man, no matter the age difference or incompatible sexuality. 'Anyway, I know what must be done.'

Nora wore a look of smug satisfaction and waited for someone to ask after her brilliant plan. My poor Arthur couldn't handle the tension and played right into her hands. 'What must be done, Nora?'

'Well, it's as they say, if you can't beat 'em, join 'em,' she said, having come around behind the desk to drape an arm around each of us. 'Neither of you will see me on your own. I can appreciate if you wish to remain faithful to each other. So, my solution: you can both come over together! I just know we'll have a wonderful time.'

'That's...' Arthur started, but seemed unable or unwilling respond any further. I had a few choice words I could supply, but I wouldn't be the one to upset this overeager older woman.

'Yes, that's settled,' Nora said, giving us each a squeeze. I can have confidence that was not where I think Arthur was going with his aborted sentence. 'I haven't had two in *such* a long time, but don't you boys worry, I'm sure I'll manage.'

This whole situation was feeling rather familiar...

Sam stepped in and said, 'Unfortunately, I have recently had a similar offer rejected. I don't think they are open to including us of the fairer sex.' You could see she meant to let the old lady down gently, but was highly amused by the situation.

Nora's soaring hopes were dashed. 'Perhaps, just as a spectator then...'

'No, they weren't having any of that either.'

The older – much older – lady looked crestfallen. 'It's just not to be,' she said with a sigh.

'No,' Sam said, still consoling. 'I'm afraid not.'

Nora took another deep breath and put on a valiant smile. 'Well, I'm happy for you Arthur, I truly am.'

'You'll have to pester some other poor bugger now, Nora,' Desmond said.

'Well, there is that new gardener Brenda's hired – quite dishy,' Nora said, her sense of determination returning with a rush.

'Or, might I suggest a more seasoned fellow?' Desmond said quietly, colour coming into his cheeks as he locked eyes with Nora. 'More seasoned, but still in his sexual prime – don't you worry about that.'

Nora blinked once and maintained eye contact.

The moment stretched on in silence. But then her lip quirked into her notorious sly smile, and Desmond smiled in response.

Charles cleared his throat and said a little louder than necessary, 'But yes, we are all happy for you, Arthur. Gabriel seems like a lovely young man.'

'I admit, I still don't understand the uh – the mechanics,' Gladys said. 'But I'm sure it must work – somehow. Seems very popular these days.'

The gruff-looking Gerry shook his head. 'Arthur, you look happy. Much more at ease, despite Nora's predatory behaviour. I am very happy for you.' The older man wrapped Arthur in a firm hug. His eyes glistened again, and he smiled as he looked to me over Gerry's shoulder.

I was happy for him too. He'd needed to do this. And surprise surprise, they had his back. They might not get it, but they loved him and he loved them.

Desmond – his complexion settled now – was the last to sum up after Arthur's coming out had been derailed a number of times.

The old man stepped forwards and shook Arthur's hand. 'Well done, lad. You too, Gabriel. Now, I don't see how you could pass up the charms of a lovely lady – Nora, or Samantha here, for example' – the women nodded appreciatively – 'but whatever gets you going, that's what I say.' He waggled his eyebrows and chuckled. 'And this Gabriel here must be doing the trick.'

Arthur apparently couldn't help but grin. 'He is indeed.'

Desmond laughed again and said, 'An added bonus: no whoopsies. You can go at it all you like and don't have to worry yourselves with a little tyke coming along in nine months.'

Charles, Gerry, and Nora laughed at that.

'But…' Gladys said, 'where does the—'

'Right,' Arthur said, not in the mood to enlighten the bewildered woman further. 'I'd better get you lot back to the tees for another swing – get your money's worth. Let's go!'

They were happy to be shepherded away, Sam joined them too, having not had a hit yet herself.

I noticed Gerry lingering a moment – it was only us two in the reception area now. He approached me at the desk, all humour having disappeared, and looked me in the eye. 'That Arthur, he's a special young man.'

'He is.'

'You will look after our Arthur, won't you?'

'I will.'

'We won't have you breaking his heart.'

'I promise I won't.'

His eyes narrowed. 'You can't promise that.'

I paused, uncertain how to respond, then said, 'I promise I will do my best.'

He nodded once, slowly. 'That's all I ask,' he said before turning to go.

I watched him rejoin the others, the way they laughed and had each other's backs. The way they meddled in each other's lives which sometimes bordered on harassment, but also showed that each person *mattered*. Like a big, extended, adopted family.

I'd been concerned that I'd moved away from my own – to gain some independence and build my own life – and that by dating Arthur, I was in danger of being swallowed up by an even bigger and more oppressive group of people.

Perhaps it just showed that they cared, and maybe that wasn't so bad.

# Chapter 7
# Isn't that what a stag do
# is all about?

## ARTHUR

We'd only just left, but Richard's grin was growing by the second. Not a harmless closed-mouth smile of contentment or even a toothy beam of joy… No, this was his signature mischievous smirk of delight. It could only mean one thing: trouble.

'Richard,' I said, putting on my sternest, most commanding voice.

'Arthur,' he said, his voice light with amusement like he didn't know precisely what I was about to ask.

'Where are we going?'

'Yeah, where are you taking us, Rich?' Nick said from the back seat. Lean and scruffy, a mess of ginger hair with a beard to match, he was wearing torn black jeans, and a faded black tee of some metal band I'd never heard of.

'This had better be worth us getting the day off for, you

prick.' That was Jason, Richard's other workmate in the back seat. Chunkier, with short brown hair and perhaps two days' worth of stubble. He was decked out like he was expecting a day in the bush or on the work site – I couldn't decide which. Orange and brown camouflage fleece top, heavy-duty grey workshop trousers, and black lace-up boots. 'Old Howard really turned it up – you know how he is – making a big song-and-dance of giving us leave. I've got weeks stacked up. But, to be fair to the old bastard, he's four men down, all on the same day and with only a couple days' notice too.'

'Don't you boys worry yourselves,' Richard said, still looking pleased with himself. 'You'll have a good time. But if you want, I can drop you off at the workshop? Old Man Howie would *love* to have you back for the day.'

'Don't you fucking dare, mate,' Nick said with a laugh as he thumped Richard's headrest.

'We're already on the way to where ever we're bloody well going, you might as well tell us,' Jason said.

The groom-to-be turned his smirk on me for a moment, then flashed it in the rear-view mirror at Nick and Jason before returning his attention to the road. 'That, my dear friends, is for me to know, and for you to find out.'

'Bah! Better be good.'

'Another surprise activity…' I said quietly, groaning to myself.

'Not just the one,' Richard said, having overheard me. 'Why'd you think I got you lot to get the day off? I have an entire *programme* of activities.'

I groaned again.

'You worried you're going to have too much fun, Artie-farts?'

I attempted a smile, but it came out more like a grimace. I'd had my fill of surprise activities this week.

Now, I'm no grinch, but being tricked into visiting Gabriel's workplace with all my honorary grandparents in tow – I hadn't been prepared for that, to come out, not in quite such a hurry. Though, I have thought on it since… Perhaps it was for the best… Let's be honest, I might never have found the *right time*. Is there even such a thing?

I had to rip the plaster off – a short, sharp pain, then it was over.

Though, having the decision taken from me rankled. Still, that wasn't really the issue, and Desmond hadn't taken us to Topdrive with any wicked intent. I had merely been led – innocently, unknowingly – right to the precipice. But no one had pushed… I jumped. And I took some pride in that.

I wasn't sure what I'd expected to happen a couple of days ago, but I know it went better than I'd feared. Introducing Gabriel to my adopted extended family as my boyfriend, well, my heart grew three sizes that night.

And with that to buoy me, I wouldn't let another unsettling surprise get to me. I refused to be the one to spoil Richard's final day as an unmarried man, which would no doubt brim with testosterone-fuelled revelry. This was his big day – well, one big day before another big day – and I was going to make sure it was all about my good friend Richard.

'No such thing as too much fun,' I said, determined to get into the spirit.

Richard crowed. 'That's my boy.'

'You do know, though,' I said, 'the whole point of a stag party is to stitch up the groom-to-be. Traditionally the job of the Best Man – in this case, me and Jared. Today is supposed to be a surprise – preferably an unpleasant one – for *you*.'

'Yeah, you've robbed us,' Jason said.

'Cool your jets, boys,' Richard said. 'You could say Lucy and I sprung this wedding on you at such short notice that you'd never have had a chance to organise anything.'

'Well—' I started, not sure what I was going to say before Richard continued.

'Anything worthwhile, that is... Arthur, I love you, you know that. And you deserve the honest answer: any stag do you organised would've been a bit shit.'

Richard's workmates in the back seat burst into laughter, and Richard held up a hand to stave off my defence.

'I know you like to keep things low-key, and I'm all about having a few pints at the pub. But this is my *stag do*. A once-in-a-lifetime opportunity, and I will not accept anything low-key.'

'But...' I couldn't argue with that – it was his bachelor party after all. I still had one concern, however: 'But, it's Friday – you do realise your wedding is tomorrow, right?'

'That's why we're starting so early!' he said. 'After a big day, and you know I mean that' – the boys in the back cheered – 'we'll be dead to the world nice and early tonight. Respectable! Then we'll be up and powering through our crippling hangovers by sparrow's fart, fresh as daisies in time to say "I do."'

I wasn't convinced.

'Don't worry grasshopper,' Richard said, slapping me on the knee. 'You know how women dream of their wedding day, have done ever since they were little girls? The flowers, the venue, the music, the colour palette – all that nonsense?'

'Yeah…'

'Well! Ever since I was a little lad, I have dreamed of my stag do. It's going to be something.'

I believed him.

'Trust me, I've thought this through.'

And that's what I was worried about.

***

We were on the outskirts of town – passing through a semi-industrial, semi-rural area – when we pulled into the Super Thrills Kart Raceway.

I clambered out of Richard's truck to the tormented whine of tiny engines being squeezed for all they were worth, shifting pitch as the karts flew past us down the straight. The squeal of tyres hanging on to the racetrack as drivers threw their karts around the sharp bends.

'How's the serenity?' Richard said, a manic grin plastered across his face.

Jared pulled into the parking space next to us, and Ben – another of Richard's workmates – jumped out, followed by Kyle and Steve – Richard's twin cousins. Richard had admitted to us they were the obligatory family invites, but you could tell they were nervously excited to be included. Jared's carload joined us in leaning over the fence to watch the racing. Each and every one of us was sporting a boyish grin – myself included.

'Ah, smell that?' Jared said once we were all gathered, taking in a deep breath and letting it out again with satisfaction. 'Two-stroke.'

We rushed into the raceway's clubhouse, raring to go, only to have the brakes slammed on by a dejected desk jockey wielding lengthy waiver forms – my second this week. Then, sat in front of a grainy TV set, we endured a safety briefing video twice as long as it needed to be and at least a decade out of date – the usual.

With that done, we signed and returned the waiver in exchange for our overalls and helmets.

'*This* is more like it,' Ben said, stepping into the legs of his overalls. I couldn't remember much about him, except for his tendency to induce groans with his asinine sense of humour and general inability to read the room. If anyone was going to make a fool of themselves tomorrow at the wedding, my bets were on Ben.

Richard's cousins, on the other hand: quiet, reserved, not likely to cause a fuss. They hadn't spoken a word yet today, and appeared to be assembled primarily of limbs – lanky and gangly, barely even real adults yet. Awkward. Though they were in their early twenties, apparently. The twins were still struggling into their overalls when the rest of us were already kitted out and at the window, watching another group of amateurs roaring around the track. I glanced back a couple of times and considered giving them a hand – it really wasn't that difficult – but their looks of determination stopped me. I wasn't going to whip away that last shred of self-respect they were clinging to in front of their big, cool cousin and his mates. They'd lose that during the first race anyway – I'd let them hold on to it a little longer.

\*\*\*

'Arthur,' Nick said as we made our way along the track to the starting grid, the kart engines left running from the previous race. 'I hear you do OK behind the wheel?'

'Yeah, not too bad,' I said. 'We've been here a few times – it's good fun.'

'*Not too bad*?' Jared said. 'Arthur's a machine! Though, I did almost beat him that one time.'

'Operative word being *almost*,' I said with a smirk.

'All right, you cocky bastard,' Jared said to me, kicking my kart before climbing into his own. 'Get in there, mate.'

'That's what she said,' Ben said, calling out over the sound of the engines.

'That was weak, Benny Boy,' Jared said. 'You're better than that.'

'Hah! No, he's not!' Richard shouted back over his shoulder from his position diagonally in front of me. 'Plus, if Arthur's getting *in* anywhere, "That's what *he* said" might be more accurate.' He shifted around in his seat enough to give me a wink and a thumbs up.

Any chance he got… I couldn't help rolling my eyes. Though, it was no worse of a ribbing than they dished out to each other. It meant they didn't care either way – my sexuality was just another laddish arrow in their quiver of boisterous banter.

Richard had told his cousins and workmates I was gay when we met up this morning, like it was no big deal. 'You remember my boy Arthur? Good mate from school. He's sharing Best Man duties with Jared on Saturday. A gay Best Man *and* a straight Best Man – diversity! Oh, Arthur's the gay one, by the way. Scored himself a fit bloke just the other day, too.' No ceremony or fanfare – just a quick update, bringing them all up to speed since he knew I hadn't seen the others in a while.

They'd taken the revelation without comment – perhaps

the odd raised eyebrow, but nothing more. After that, four of us had piled into Richard's truck, the rest into Jared's car, and off we went.

'Fuck off, Richard,' I said – the only valid response to any 'that's what he or she said' comment.

He smiled and revved his kart. 'Listen to that – singing like a bird.'

I smiled back at him, then settled into my seat, familiarising myself with the grip of the steering wheel, the give of the pedals, the feel of the rumbling little rocket beneath me. I was already starting to heat up in my overalls and found my mind drifting as we waited for the others to strap themselves in and get comfortable. Would Gabriel enjoy this? I didn't think he was a big motorhead or anything… But then, neither was I – cars got you from A to B, nothing to get excited about – but kart racing… What a rush! Quick, fast, competitive. It didn't hurt that I happened to be pretty good at it, too.

Karting wasn't your usual date activity, but I decided I'd have to bring him some time. Not that I wanted to get ahead of myself. It was still early days, but dating Gabriel had prompted an upheaval in my closeted yet contented life. The more I stopped hiding this part of me from my people, the more I wanted to share him with those same people. I wished he was here now…

I was so wrapped up reflecting on hefty life changes and foreign feelings that I almost missed the start of the race. The lights were flashing at the start line – I barely had my hands back on the wheel and my feet on the pedals when the green light signalled the start of our race. The high-pitched scream of tiny engines blasted as we shot over the starting line as one.

'What's got into you today, Artie-farts?' Jared said, pulling off his helmet. 'Those fumes smoked your motor skills? You weren't your best out there.'

'That's putting it lightly,' Richard said, following us into the clubhouse.

'Nothing.' I couldn't admit I'd rather be spending time with Gabriel. Pathetic, really. And not cool – bros before hoes, mates before dates, all that. 'I just—'

'I lapped you, Arthur,' Jared said. '*Lapped* you. As in, I was an *entire* lap ahead of—'

'Yes, thank you Jared, I know what *being lapped* means.' I hadn't meant to snap, but I couldn't help myself.

'I think even one of Richard's cousins passed you. Was that you, Steve?' Jared said to the twins, then continued before either could respond. 'I can't tell them apart... That's beside the point, neither of them even have their Full Driver Licences yet. And one of them passed—'

'He gets the picture.' Jason – the first race victor – waved Jared quiet.

'Day-dreaming then, were we?' Richard said. 'Has all the excitement and romance of my impending nuptials and stag do got you hearing wedding bells?'

'Uh?' No, but he wasn't so far off the mark. 'No, it's not—'

'You thinking about Gabey-baby?' Richard said in a lovey-dovey tone.

Damn.

'Is that the boyfriend?' Nick said, tying off the arms of his overalls around his waist as he joined us at the window to watch the other group of amateurs race. They'd scheduled us for alternate races, giving each group a breather in between.

'Sure is,' Richard said. 'You'll meet him at the wedding. Our Arthur plucked up the courage to invite a plus-one.'

'Finally!' Jared said.

'I get it – budding romance and so on and so forth – he is quite the catch,' Richard said with a grin. 'And it's a big step, having him on your arm at an *event* – makes it official. Now, Arthur,' Richard said, hand on my shoulder. 'I hate to make this about me… but it is *all* about me. Today we commemorate the conclusion of my bachelorhood, and tomorrow we celebrate my marriage. I am the groom and I pull rank: today is my stag do and so I say today we race.'

'Eyes on the prize, my man,' Jason said to me. 'I want some real competition for the next race.'

'For sure,' Nick said, punching Jason in the shoulder. 'Someone had better beat this prick or he won't be able to fit his head back in that helmet.'

'Knock him down a peg or two, will you, Arthur?' Richard said. 'For me?'

'Head in the game!' Jared said, emphasised with a slap on my shoulder.

'And to do that,' Richard said, 'we can't be having you distracted.'

'Or… dick-stracted,' Ben said, with a smirk. 'Get it? Because he's too busy thinking about dick.'

'Hah! Maybe you need to imagine *that* will be your prize,' Nick said, with a wink at me. 'To help motivate you.'

'That good is it?' Jason said, part-joking, but part-proud for me.

I knew I'd gone red, which only fuelled their obscene glee.

Once they'd satisfied themselves I was well and truly dying of embarrassment, Jared said to Richard, 'Why don't we invite him?'

'What?' I said, unsure I'd heard right.

Richard nodded and shrugged, like he couldn't believe he hadn't thought of it himself.

'You call Gabriel,' Jared said, 'and tell him to get that butt of his you like so much and bring it here.'

'Why – but – why would...'

'If you're going to stare into the distance, all doe-eyed like, instead of driving properly, invite him!' Richard said. 'Then you can stop pining, and maybe you'll be able to concentrate—'

'Dick-stracted,' Ben said, matter-of-fact.

'Yes, thank you, Benny Boy, we heard you the first time,' Jason said.

'It's a stag do! You two may be shagging, but he's still a guy,' Richard said. 'He should be at my stag do – it's traditional.'

'Uh—'

'What are you worried about now, Arthur?' Richard said. 'That he's going to show us all how much more of a man he is than you are?'

'Oh, *yes*. That's what we need,' Nick said, rubbing his hands together. 'A healthy dose of toxic masculinity to get his stag do pumping.'

Richard laughed. 'Isn't that what a stag do is all about? Blast out the last of my childish, misogynist ways, before transforming into a well-adjusted gentleman in time for a life of marital bliss?'

'And it won't be a second too soon,' Jared said.

'Just get him here,' Richard said. 'I like him – he's good

for you. And he's hot too. That'll be good for' – he nodded down at my crotch – 'you know.'

'Dick-tastic!' Ben said.

'Ben,' Jason said, 'who invited you, anyway?'

I wasn't listening anymore.

Richard nodded and said to me quietly, 'Go on, get him to meet us later – he's not working today, right?'

I shook my head.

'He can join us for the next *activity*,' Richard said with a smile and a nudge before showing me the address. 'He'll love it.'

So much for me not dampening spirits or detracting from Richard's last day as a 'bachelor'. I was doing a shocking job, making this whole bloody thing about myself with my half-arsed driving. I knew I wasn't *present*, and that wasn't fair on my friend. And here he was, turning it around to make me happy. I couldn't very well be some absent moron, then go and reject his offer…

Richard caught my eye and nodded again before returning his attention to the racing and the others giving each other a ribbing.

I sighed, rubbed my face, and pulled out my phone to draft a message, smiling but anxious. And before I could second guess myself, I sent it.

# Chapter 8
# An invitation to the bro-fest?

**GABRIEL**

I sat slumped over on my duvet, head resting on the desk which overhung the end of my bed. I stared out the window, blowing another sigh which sent the pages of my course notes fluttering – I'd lost track of how long I'd been right here, doing just this.

The wedding was tomorrow, but today was wide open. I had no classes and no work at the driving range. Claire and Theo were out of the flat, Betty and Basil were napping in their usual spots, and Arthur was busy at Richard's bachelor party. I had perfect silence, no distractions – the ideal studying conditions.

So, of course I couldn't. Not a chance. Despite my shortage of distractions, my attention was still drawn elsewhere. No points for guessing what – or more accurately, who – I was thinking about.

I'd cracked open my laptop, course notes, and a textbook – but that's as far as I'd got. I'd been determined to use this day to get ahead. With no tests or submissions due in the next week or so, I could really cement what I'd learnt so far, put me in good stead for the end-of-semester exams. Take the pressure off during the exam break, avoid the frantic last minute cramming.

I was starting early – heeding the advice that had been drummed into us all through school. If I was to be classified – however unfairly – as a *mature* student, the least I could do was *act* mature.

But there's really nothing quite like a rapidly approaching deadline to fire you up, is there? To focus the mind.

Having all the time in the world and so-called 'ideal' working conditions was overrated. A tight deadline – that's when shit gets done.

I was reflecting on the unhelpfulness of the well-meant advice when my head buzzed – something happening! I shot up to see the new notification on my phone.

*Hey. I'm at Richard's stag do. Kart racing. Do you want to join us afterwards?*

What was this – an invitation to the bro-fest? I hadn't expected to hear from Arthur today. Thought he'd be too busy ladding it up with the boys – Richard's last hurrah and all that.

After my brief intermission considering the merits of procrastination, the message had yanked my mind back to Arthur. I was coming to realise that he liked to know what was going on, preferred a bit of routine. I expect this week was his worst nightmare… Taking random days off work, getting dragged to unknown activities. For someone so disorganised, he had an astonishing aversion to surprises.

But back to the message: did I want to join them? Not so

much – these guys weren't my mates, not really, not yet anyway. Plus-ones go to the wedding, not the stag do.

Though, I did want to see Arthur…

I scolded myself – I'd be seeing him tomorrow. And from the little I knew of Richard, he'd be going all out today. No way did I want to be lurching to the wedding, looking like death and nursing a hangover as I suffered through the ceremony and small talk with strangers. It could be done, but why would I if I could help it? I am *mature*, remember?

Regardless, I'd be setting a dangerous precedent, having Arthur thinking he could summon me at the drop of a hat. No, start as you intend to continue.

I'm busy.

I picked up my phone to say as much when it vibrated again.

*I'm really sorry, I know it's short notice and you don't have to come if you don't want to.*

Well, at least he's self-aware.

Perhaps I *could* go along today without him coming to expect it in future? As long as I didn't let it happen again. I didn't want to encourage this kind of behaviour…

I re-read the messages. It almost read like he didn't want me to come – had Richard put him up to this? Was I part of the entertainment? I didn't see how – straight boys were all about the busty lady strippers, weren't they? But I wouldn't put it past that friend of Arthur's to come up with something obscene – he was shameless. No, I don't think Arthur actually wanted—

*I would like it if you did come.*

Well, shit. So much for that thinking. Still bloody presumptuous of—

*Only if you're free, though. I know you're busy.*

This boy had an answer for everything, and I hadn't even responded yet.

Who was I kidding? I wasn't getting any studying done. Arthur wanted me with him, I wanted to be with him – what was there to think about?

Arthur's anxiousness was rubbing off on me.

I smiled.

He *was* anxious – why else would he send a flurry of follow-up messages? Even so, I noticed he never let himself send anything with typos. I'd never known someone to be so diligent with their apostrophes.

I smiled again, I'd better put him out of his misery:

*Sounds great, it'll be a riot. When and where?*

\*\*\*

An hour later, I pulled up to a pub on the edge of town. A couple of locals were stationed outside, rough-looking old boys having a smoke with their pints. They watched me get out and head for the front door.

I nodded, they nodded back. All was well.

I ducked through the front door to find the interior was as well worn and hard-nosed as the sentries outside.

There were a few others scattered around the place – some watching the sport on TV, another trying his luck on the machines, the rest quietly having their beers.

Richard though, he was in full swing, regaling all who would listen with what sounded like a triumphant tale, punctuated with impressively authentic racing car noises. He was surrounded by a few scruffy guys who were about our age – presumably the workmates – two timid beanstalks nervously sipping their pints, as well as Jared and Arthur. I couldn't help but smile at the sight of him.

'And then he shot past like – Gabey-baby! There he is,' Richard said, cutting off his animated anecdote to rush over and give me a big bear hug. Not one of those millisecond hugs followed by much back slapping – the straight man's favoured embrace which said, 'Great to see you, man. Love you to bits. But let's not be gay about it.' No, Richard gave me a proper hug, not worried the gay would rub off on him – he went up another notch in my books.

He stank, though. 'The kart racing hard work, was it?'

'They bloody well didn't drive themselves, I'll tell you that much,' Richard said. 'Worked up a sweat in those heavy overalls.'

'You don't say,' I said with a smirk.

'Don't you worry,' Richard said with a slap on the back. 'You'll be as fragrant as the rest of us after our next fixture.'

The groom-to-be turned to introduce me to the guys from his work, and his cousins – the spindly pair.

I'd shaken everyone's hand before Richard presented Arthur, like he was the grand prize. 'And I believe you've met my Best Man—'

'Joint Best Man,' Jared said with a smile and a toast to himself.

'Yes, my *joint* Best Man, Arthur Pendragon – no, hang on, that's not right... Arthur Fenwick! Not so royal, but today he was legendary, all right.'

Arthur's tentative smile grew a little proud.

I stepped in to give him a hello hug, just like I'd received from Richard – I dared not go in for anything more intimate, doubtful I'd get an agreeable reception. As much as I wanted to, it just wouldn't be in keeping with the vibe of the place – not a sequin curtain, two-for-one cocktail special, or little rainbow flag in sight.

I leaned in for the conventional hug, common to all huggers of comparable height: left arms under, right arms over, heads to the left over the other's shoulder. The perfect clash-free option.

And it would've gone perfectly, but before I could get my arms around him Arthur had dived in for a kiss. It only lasted a second, and I was too shocked to reciprocate before he stepped back again, his face flushing red as the boys cheered and whooped and laughed.

'Get in there, mate!'

'Give it to him!'

'Bah! Get a room.'

'Is that all you got, bro?'

They quietened down quickly as they took another gulp of their beers – ribbing was thirsty work. Richard handed me a full pint they'd grabbed before I arrived.

'He's been pining for you all day, Gabes,' Jared said.

Arthur spluttered. 'I have not—'

'Yeah, he has – embarrassing, really. Severely impacted his performance on the track,' Richard said with a shake of the head. 'We couldn't have that. The second you responded to say you were coming, it's like he was a new man.'

Arthur flushed harder, though I noticed he wasn't attempting to deny it now.

'I lapped him in the first race,' Jared said. '*Lapped!* Unheard of.'

'Then he summoned his sweet, sweet love,' Richard said, lips pursed, looking at me and blinking like he was in a mascara commercial. 'And *voilà*! Mr Lightning McFenwick was back.'

'Still, didn't beat me in the second race, did he?' Nick

said.

'A close second,' Richard conceded. 'But then he smashed us in that third race – untouchable.'

'So, Gabriel,' Jared said. 'With a seventh, second, and a first, your neurotic loverboy took out the top spot.'

'Champion!' Richard shouted, squeezing Arthur by the shoulder.

'That so?' I said. I had to admit, I hadn't picked him as the competitive type, or someone able to handle a vehicle with any finesse.

Arthur nodded, flustered by the attention.

'You'll have to take your boyfriend for a victory lap later,' Nick said to Arthur with a smirk. 'Show him how a champion does it.'

Arthur tried to object, 'What does that even—'

'Later,' Richard said, holding a hand up. '*Much* later. Now, Gabriel' – he levelled a finger at me – 'I trust you won't be stealing Arthur from us tonight?'

'I wouldn't dare' – laughing as I put my hand on my heart – 'I'll make sure Arthur is devoted to any and all Best Man duties this evening.'

'Good. See, Arthur? Why can't you be more like your boyfriend? Focused! Dedicated to the cause! I've got too much planned, and we've just got your mind back on the task at hand. As much as I approve of this union,' Richard said, gesturing between me and Arthur, 'I can't be having you two on heat, sneaking off for a rut in the corner every five minutes.'

Arthur had already reached peak embarrassment – he took this without comment, downing the rest of his pint instead and setting it back on the table.

While Arthur drowned in awkwardness, Jason was

arching his back in a stretch.

'Yeah,' Nick said. 'Those karts were a fair workout.'

'No power steering,' Jared said, like he knew what he was talking about. 'Was heavier than driving my truck.'

'My arms, shoulders, back,' Ben said. 'Really going to feel it tomorrow.'

'I can barely lift this pint glass,' Jason said. 'And it's almost empty.'

'I'm sure we'll find the strength,' Richard said, raising his glass for a toast.

'But, you know,' Jared said with a shrug and a cocky wink, 'this rig can handle more than some little kiddie kart.'

'Oh, fuck off,' Richard said. 'You're not feeling it because you were driving like your great aunt, easing that kart around the corners like you were out for a Sunday drive. It was shameful, really.'

'My big shoulders could barely fit in the seat,' Jared said. 'Limited my range of movement. Can't help it if I'm tank.'

'Mate, you're full of it,' Jason said. 'Anyway, next round?'

'Nope!' Richard said, something I'd never expected to hear from him. 'Just the one here, boys. Next engagement first. Can't be too pissed or we'll be no bloody good. Then after that, all bets are off. But we'd better get going – down the last of those pints.'

Most had already finished, but the twins – Kyle and Steve – still had half a glass each. They valiantly downed their pints, and we headed out the door.

'I hope you bastards put on your thickest skins this morning,' Richard said with a manic grin. 'Because this is going to *hurt*.'

***

And hurt it did. More so for Richard than the rest of us, but we still copped our fair share.

If I thought these guys were ripe after the kart racing, I hated to think what we all smelt like now. But Richard was right. I must've been as bad as the others if I didn't notice that post-match changing room stench anymore.

The others were kitted out in their second pair of overalls for the day – my first – as we traversed the heavily vegetated valley, with plastic helmets and visors strapped to our heads, and semi-automatic, compressed gas-powered guns in our grasps.

Paintballs had started flying the second the whistle blew for our first round of *Capture the Flag*. The aim of the game: protect your fort and its flag while attempting to steal your opposition's flag and return it to your own fort.

Simple in theory, painful in practise.

They pitted me and Arthur against each other by assigning us to opposing teams. 'Can't have you boys hiding out in the bush, you know? Shooting your loads instead of shooting each other,' Richard said. 'No, better to have you on different teams.'

Arthur protested. 'We're not going to—'

'Good to hear!' Richard said with a laugh. 'Or I'll shoot your dick off.'

Arthur had rolled his eyes and gave me a tight smile.

Kyle and Steve were split up too. The reasoning Richard voiced was the twins' psychic connection would give them an unfair competitive advantage if they were on the same side. In reality, he thought they'd suck big time and didn't want one team lumped with both dead weights.

This couldn't have been further from the truth. The twins were avid gamers, with a heavy preference for some first-person shooter I'd never heard of. It was no doubt bloody and violent, the type of game abhorred by pearl-clutching busybodies the world over. But it gave these weedy cousins of Richard's the theory needed to mount a successful incursion.

Kyle transformed in front of my eyes, taking charge – he speaks! – as soon as we were out of earshot of the opposition, laying out strategies and counter-strategies to circumvent the ploys his brother would likely attempt. Richard was too shocked to interrupt, shrugging when I looked his way. His shoulders said, 'Why not?' From what I knew of Richard, his 'plan' would've been to storm through the guts and hope for the best.

Nick and Ben rounded out my team – the reds – bringing us to five. Arthur, Jared, Jason, and Steve made up the blue team. My last minute addition had skewed the team sizes, but Jason had real-life hunting experience, so it was decided that the team with him on it ought to be the smaller one.

Kyle defended our fort with unnerving efficiency, picking off any attempt on our flag. The rest of us surged forwards on the offence, clambering up and down the valley slopes, dashing from tree to shrub to fallen log, snatching the blue flag and getting it back to our fort before even Jason had laid a hand on our red flag.

'Good stuff, guys,' Kyle said when our team was all back at the base.

Richard sneaked behind his cousin, ducked his head through Kyle's legs and stood upright, parading him around the base on his shoulders as the losing team trickled in. Initially indignant, the victorious twin was soon beaming with pride.

I caught Arthur's eye briefly. He looked like he'd been run ragged, but he was having fun, his small smile of amusement jumping wider when he saw me looking. Maybe it was a good thing Richard had separated us. With blood pumping, heavy breathing and all that, I was feeling things.

But I didn't have long to reflect on this, as we were only back at base for a few minutes. We grabbed drinks of water, refilled our hoppers and spare canisters with paintballs, and briefly relived the highlights of the first round before we were back out there.

The next rounds were *King of the Hill* and *Total Domination*. The twins put us to shame each time. It was surprisingly satisfying, seeing them run circles around Richard's workmates who'd thought they were all that with a paintball gun.

The organised games were finished now – I checked my hopper and found it was still half-full of unused prepaid paintballs, obviously too successful in my ammunition conservation.

'Right lads,' the guy in charge of the place said. 'I hear this is a stag do.'

This was met with cheers and hoots and grunts from the 'hunters'.

'Who's the unlucky man, then?'

We all stepped back from Richard, who was looking rather proud of himself. 'That'd be me,' he said.

'Right, then,' the manager said. 'Strip! Down to those tighty-whities.'

'What?' Richard said with a laugh, looking around at the rest of us before returning his attention to the manager.

'Sorry mate, I'm not really an in-public kind of guy. Besides, you're not my type.'

'Keep your knickers on,' the manager said with a smirk. 'Literally. We don't want to see your bits. But we need you ready for the final game. I hope everyone has at least a handful of paintballs left?'

Everyone popped the lids on their hoppers as I'd done only a minute ago, followed by knowing smiles all round.

'This final game we call *The Last Gasp of Freedom*,' the manager said. 'Our groom-to-be runs the length of the obstacle field, one end to the other and back again. Simple, right? And you lot, his good mates, will be lining the course emptying those hoppers.'

'Don't worry, buddy,' Jared said. 'We'll be sure to avoid the wedding tackle. Lucy would never forgive us if that was out of action on the big night.'

Richard tried to laugh it off, but it was obvious he was struggling to keep his brave face on.

'All right Casanova, let's see that flesh,' the manager said. 'Get your kit off. Helmet back on, though – health and safety, you know.'

'Don't want you getting any balls to the face,' Arthur said, looking sly.

'You'd love that, wouldn't you? Dirty prick,' Richard said, an automatic response. Though it had served to distract the groom-to-be from the impending pain – if only briefly.

I'd taken a few body shots during the games. The overalls were thick, but each hit stung like a bastard – the paintballs didn't even burst half the time. I knew the impacts would show up later.

Poor Richard, he wouldn't even have that layer of fabric

any more. He was going to be polka dotted with bruises after this if he was lucky, welts if he wasn't. And to think I'd been worried about bruising from those golf balls Sheela lobbed at me – laughable.

The final game went as expected, and I managed to get a couple of my dye-filled capsules on target. One burst and one didn't – a green splotch evidence of the first hit, and a big block of purple bruise appearing in the next few days would be evidence of the second. I grimaced at the thought.

Richard roared the length of the obstacle field and back, ducking behind upright wooden pallets, empty oil drums, and stacks of car tyres as much as he could. Covered in splotches, and hunched over with hands on knees at the end, he declared that it was time for a drink.

And so we were back at the pub. We were fully clothed, and I'm sure we smelt fouler than ever, but Richard had regained his good humour.

'Cheers, boys,' Richard said, raising his fresh pint. 'To my cousins – who knew they had it in them?'

We all gave a roar of approval, and the twins still looked sheepish but also a little proud.

A few rounds later, with the alcohol working nicely on everyone's aches and pains, the others were too distracted to notice when Arthur stepped up close to me again. The first time had resulted in a round of kissy-grunty noises from the others, so he'd kept his distance after that for fear of setting them off again. But they weren't paying attention anymore.

'You know, today's been fun,' Arthur said to me – quiet and confidential – as if admitting he'd girded himself for the worst, then found it was in fact not the worst.

I agreed, happy he was enjoying himself.

'And I'm glad you came.'

'I'm glad I did, too.' I couldn't help but smile at his earnestness, and how far he'd come already. Willing to bring me out – his same-sex lover. He'd dragged himself out of the closet in frustration with his best mates the first time around. The second big time had been thrust upon him with the pensioners, lest he deny me right to my face. But today, well, he invited me along all by himself to hang out with a bunch of lads – not the type often counted as rainbow allies.

'Kart racing, paintball, then a few pints at the pub. All round, a good day out,' Arthur said, nodding along. 'For sure bachelor party fodder, but you've met Richard – I was all ready for some near-apocalypse grade antics.'

I laughed. 'Paintball was almost civilised in comparison. Not my go-to for fun, but I had a good time. And everyone's still in one piece for the wedding tomorrow.'

'Right! You know what I mean, though? I was ready for a riding of the bulls level shit show.'

I couldn't help the short burst of laughter. Blame the booze – we certainly wouldn't be driving home tonight. 'It's *running* of the bulls.'

'Is it?' Arthur paused a moment, looking confused. 'Well, if Richard was in charge we'd have been riding them, don't you worry about that.'

'I can't disagree with that.'

'Or, if not that, he'd have had us doing something else equally ridiculous and life-threatening,' Arthur said, pint in hand and gesturing wildly, beer spilling over anyone who dared get near. Then he looked at me like he'd had a thought. 'Have you heard of that cheese rolling competition?'

'What? No. I do love cheese, though,' I said. 'But what's

the—'

'You see, what they do is they go – they go to the top of some steep hill in the countryside. They do it every year, you know? Annual event.'

'Yes, sure,' I said after Arthur paused to check I was following. I couldn't help myself from adding, 'Annual events famously occur every year.'

'They do, don't they?'

'Yes, Arthur.' I was starting to think we needed to get some food in this lot, perhaps after this story. 'Anyway, what's the event?'

'What event?'

'The *annual* event. Cheese rolling, was it?'

'Oh, yeah! Guys, have you heard of this?' Arthur said, cutting across the others to get their attention, clearly having forgotten the reason for this story.

'What's that, mate?' Jared said.

'The cheese rolling competition! They get this big fuck off wheel of Double Gloucester and send it rolling down the hill. It's bloody steep, too. Not your gentle rolling hill, might as well be a cliff. Anyway, then – then! – these idiots chase after it. First to the bottom wins the cheese. It's a whole big thing. People breaking a *lot* of shit. They even have ambulances at the end – literally at the bottom of the cliff.'

Arthur's audience was in awe.

'Bloody legends,' Jason said.

'Yeah, sounds like a blast,' Nick added.

'I reckon we could do it,' Richard said, nodding like it was the best thing he'd ever heard. 'But, that'll have to be for another day, because…'

Richard spread his arms out to clear the way as the bartender approached. In his hands he carried a huge tray covered with shot glasses, wedges of limes resting on top of each, and a big salt shaker in the middle.

'No.'

'Yes.'

'No bloody way.'

'Hell yes, buddy!'

'Tequilaaa!'

Half the group cheered, the other half groaned.

'Finish those pints first,' Richard said. 'Bottoms up.' He winked at me and Arthur, 'I mean the drinks, you dirty bastards.'

Everyone followed orders, slamming down their empty pint glasses to grab their first shots.

'To my future wife, Lucy!' Richard declared.

Cheers, salt lick, shot, lime bite, shudder.

'And to my boys!' Richard said, raising his second shot and everyone followed suit: cheers, salt lick, shot, lime bite, shudder.

'And now,' Richard said with a manic grin, his hundredth of the day it seemed, 'I have a surprise for you all.'

'What?' That was Arthur, his face a look of horror.

'You didn't think the pub was the end of the festivities, did you my dear, sweet Arthur?' Richard said. 'Have you met me?'

The groom-to-be put his arm around Arthur, leading him to the door and calling over his shoulder, 'Come on you lot! We're out of here.'

Stumbling out into the street, I heard a thump of music and hiss of brakes, then looking up I saw the psychedelic paint job and strobe disco lights of a—

'Party bus!' Richard said, beaming as he presented the

next step on his bachelor party tour. 'Get in losers, we're going partying!'

# Chapter 9
# I wasn't convinced,
# but what could I do?

**ARTHUR**

I stirred, slowly rousing from an awful sleep. My body ached, as if I'd been wrung out and dragged behind a truck down the street – a street lined with speed bumps and potholes.

Testing out my limbs with slight adjustments I became aware of something warm pressed against my front, my arm already wrapped around.

I smiled and snuggled in – I could get used to having a boyfriend. He was the little spoon, radiating heat, and cocooned entirely by me. Well, we were similarly sized spoons, stacked neatly with me behind him. It was cosy and wonderful and pleasantly distracting, enough to forget about my aching body for a moment.

I was reluctant to extricate myself from our huddle, but I desperately needed to pee. Cracking my eye open a sliver, I lifted my arm off him and grabbed the tabletop to pull myself—

The tabletop?

I opened my eyes properly, blinking away the sleep, to see what was indeed a table. And my arm, which was wearing a jacket. Why was I – I was fully clothed, as was my personal radiator, and we were lying on dark red leather. Booth seating… Where were—

A scream cut through my thoughts. I launched into an upright position and immediately felt the room slide out from underneath me, the floor shifting up to become the wall. My arms flung out on their own, catching me on the floor-wall and holding me still. The spinning of the room slowly ground to a halt, but my stomach kept going, churning around and around and around.

I clutched at my front – a futile move – it needed to get out and there was no stopping it.

The uniformed woman – presumably the source of the scream – pointed desperately away from the booth. I saw the universal sign for the toilet, lurched forwards and wrenched back the sliding door to the accessible bathroom. I braced myself on the seat in time for my stomach to launch up my throat and out my mouth. It continued clawing its way up until it felt like nothing was left.

I slumped on the floor and looked back miserably – slow movements, easy does it. I recognised the uniform now, your generic chain coffee shop costume. The barista was appalled, standing in the open doorway.

She was surrounded by a bunch of familiar faces: Jared, haunted, dark circles under his eyes; Jason, scrubbing his face with his hands; and Richard, looking like this was the best thing he'd ever seen.

I was mortified. Though, glad Gabriel hadn't witnessed that – a small mercy.

The barista walked off in disgust as I flushed away the evidence of my shame and splashed my face in the sink.

The upchuck and the cold water left me feeling marginally less rotten. 'Let's get out of here,' I said, shooing the others out of my way as I went to wake Gabriel – if my loud heaving hadn't already done that for me.

Nick and Ben were still coming to life as I left the bathroom, sitting up from their makeshift bed in the booth opposite the one I'd evacuated.

'Where's Gabriel?' I said, standing next to our now-empty booth.

'What?' Richard said, still amused but now looking a little like I'd lost my mind.

'We were in this booth,' I said, pointing beside me.

'No,' Jared said. 'That was my spot.'

It took a second, but then I blanched, realising who my little spoon was. Well, that was cosy. We were fully clothed, though, so nothing untoward.

'He must be in the bathroom, I'll go check he's all right.' I escaped the awkward moment and headed to the men's. If he was in a state like me, he might need checking on.

I barrelled in to find all the stalls empty, urinals unoccupied, and nobody at the shining white sinks either.

He wasn't out there, and he wasn't in here. The dread hit me like a punch to the guts and I keeled over, emptying more of my stomach into the sink, vomit splashing up onto the mirror.

I heaved again and again till nothing but hot bile came up. It was horrific – not just the pain, but the shame of it, and now Gabriel was missing too.

Was he OK? Was he hurt?

Where was he? Alone, abandoned, drowning in his own vomit?

I was breathing hard now, frantically mopping at the spray of sick with wetted paper towels as I crashed through all the possibilities in my pounding head.

Or had I done something? Made a complete arse of myself in front of him?

I couldn't remember anything, not since shotting that tequila and getting on the party bus. I kept mopping, the paper towels disintegrating in my hands and leaving a pulpy mess.

Had he realised I was no good, and left?

I yanked more and more paper towels from the dispenser in a desperate attempt to clean up my mess before crumpling onto the floor in great, uncontrollable sobs, tears streaming from my eyes as I clutched wads of the wet paper.

### GABRIEL

'I think that spot is done,' I heard Claire say, her voice soft and apologetic.

I snapped back from my scrutiny of the living room wall, casting my eyes down at the iron I'd been pushing back and forth across the same patch of my shirt for I don't know how long. Not trusting myself to respond, I placed the iron in its cradle without acknowledging her.

Now no longer pressed to the fabric, it hissed with steam – which was fitting, really, because I was fuming.

After a moment I shifted my shirt on the ironing board, picked up the iron again and focused on getting the rest of the creases out.

'We're both really sorry, Gabriel,' she said after I made no show of responding. 'We might have overreacted a bit.'

'A bit?' I said through gritted teeth, unable to contain myself anymore. With shaking hands I placed the iron back in its cradle, lest my arm got a mind of its own and threw the burning hot and hefty appliance across the flat.

'A bit!' That came out as a snarl and at serious volume.

Theo emerged from Claire's room behind her, hopping on one foot and balancing himself on the door frame as he rubbed his eyes. 'Sorry, mate,' he said, still half asleep. 'We didn't realise you were with Arthur at Richard's thing. Thought it was a *boys-only* thing.'

'I am a fucking boy!'

'Yes, yes. I know,' Theo said, obviously trying to keep things cool. 'But you're also a plus-one. You said you were going to be studying all day?'

'Plans changed, didn't they?' I was twitchy now, made worse by the knowledge that there was nothing I could do. I had to wait and hope and not lose my shit in frustration. The feeling was complete impotence.

'We're really sorry—'

'An "emergency", that's what you said! Missed calls from both of you, one after the other. Messages too – hang on, let me read them… "*Help! Get back to flat ASAP*". And, "*Flat emergency. Get here now.*" Followed up with, "*Now! Where are you? I don't know how long we can hold out.*"' I stared them both down. 'What the *fuck* am I supposed to think when I see messages like that? Then when I called back, no answer!'

I kept staring until they spoke.

'We panicked when they got too close,' Claire said,

thoroughly chastised. 'We dropped our phones.'

'Then they were out of reach,' Theo added, cowering, 'so we couldn't answer.'

I breathed again. We'd already gone through this last night and I needed to calm down. I just needed to get it out before we could move past it and enjoy the day – I hoped.

'*Mice* in the house is *not* an emergency. Mice!' I said. 'Now, if Theo had gone and broken his other bloody leg – *that* would be closer to an emergency. Which very well might have happened with you two lunatics squealing from on top of the dining table. But Betty and Basil bringing live mice into the flat and batting them around – granted, they've never brought any in before – but no, not an emergency.'

They nodded like chastised children who'd been caught sneaking peeks at the presents under the Christmas tree. Theo wasn't unfamiliar with getting told off, but Claire was so put together I couldn't imagine she'd been scolded in more than a decade or two. And then there was Basil, the orange lump perched on his spot on the couch back, sleeping the untroubled sleep of the innocent. Betty was present as well, sat awkwardly on a plastic bag filled with art supplies on the floor, licking herself, oblivious to the tense atmosphere.

I sighed, having had enough grinching. 'Now I'm the one overreacting, I'm sorry. It's probably fine. Arthur's probably fine. *We* are probably fine.'

Last night, after seeing all the missed calls and messages and not being able to get through to Theo or Claire, I'd left Richard's stag do. I told Arthur I had to go, and when he tried to follow I said I didn't want to cut his night short, and as Best Man – one of two – he had a responsibility to ensure the groom-to-be had a night to remember. He was reluctant for me to go, wearing a hurt look I couldn't get out of my head, and then I rushed back for what turned out to be very much a non-emergency. I evicted the tortured rodents – and the cats for good measure – so Theo and Claire could clamber sheepishly down from the dining table.

By the time I'd sorted that out I couldn't get through to Arthur, with messages unread and calls going to voicemail. The bachelor party had been moving around a fair bit, the party bus carting us from place to place. Richard was tight-lipped about the upcoming destinations, keeping each a surprise for us. They would've moved on by the time I got back. So there was no point attempting to rejoin them if I didn't know where to go – they could be anywhere.

And all I could think about was that hurt look on Arthur's face. I expect the expression was intensified by his drunkenness, but that didn't stop me seeing it.

'It'll be fine. He would've been caught up last night and forgotten to check his phone, then forgotten to charge it when he went to bed,' Claire said. 'He'll be OK – don't worry. We'll see him at the wedding.'

'Yeah…' I wasn't convinced, but what could I do? The damage was done. He'd invited me along last night, and I'd abandoned him.

'Have you tried the others?' Theo said.

'I don't have their numbers or anything,' I said. We weren't otherwise 'connected' online either. Truth is, I hardly knew them, I've been too busy getting to know Arthur. 'Would you believe we haven't even known each other for three weeks yet?'

'Fuck, is that it, Gramps? Feels like forever,' Theo said.

'You've fallen heavy and hard, haven't you?' Claire

added.

I looked down, unable to maintain eye contact with my flatmates. I picked up the iron and finished my shirt.

## ARTHUR

'Oh, mate,' Richard said, coming into the bathroom to see me a blubbering wreck on the tiles. 'Still blowing chunks, are we?'

I knew I must look a right sight, but I just couldn't bring myself to care right now.

'Calm down, will you?' he said, squatting next to me and putting an arm around my shoulders. 'What's the deal?'

I choked out Gabriel's name or something like it. Whatever I'd managed, Richard understood.

'He headed off, don't you remember?'

'What?' I said, whipping my head up and wiping my eyes with the back of my hand. 'When? Why?'

'Not sure exactly when. Can't remember most of the night, only snatches' – Richard smirked, like the bit he was remembering now tickled him enormously – 'but I do remember giving him a big farewell hug and a kiss.'

'So – so he's OK?' I said.

'Yeah, he still had his head screwed on, so he would've got back OK.'

'But, why did he—'

'Probably saw what state you were in and found himself a better offer for the night,' Richard said.

I felt my eyes and mouth go wide in horror – I knew it.

'Whoa there, boy,' Richard said, laughing. 'Just messing with you. You weren't *that* bad. Your loverboy said something about some drama or something, can't

131

remember. Was it his flatmates? Or his mum? Or was I just thinking about his mum? She'd be a nice-looking lady, I reckon, much like your lovely Denise.' Richard paused and looked back at me. 'Anyway, I remember he wasn't happy about it, nor about ditching you. But I reassured him, said you were in very capable and trustworthy hands.'

I frowned at that.

'And here you are,' he said, pulling me upright, 'alive and well.'

'Alive, perhaps,' I said.

'Look at that,' Richard said with a smile. 'Humour coming rushing back – our boy's on the mend! But we'd better go, we've already ruined that poor barista's morning. Besides, we've got a wedding to get to.'

I'd tried to catch the barista's eye as our ragtag group shuffled past to mouth an apology, but she was busying herself setting up the cafe for the morning, studiously ignoring us.

The waist height railings had still been halfway across the entrance as we left – had we scaled those to get in? Hang on, why didn't this coffee shop have a proper front door?

I stopped outside the entrance to get a look around, though careful not to give myself motion sickness. The place had that distinctive glare of polished tiled surfaces, over-eager air-conditioning, and an all round artificial quality to it. 'Did we break into a shopping centre?' I said.

'Firstly, I don't think we broke in… we were locked in,' Richard said in our defence, finger raised. Then he followed my lead and looked around. 'And this is no mall…'

'It's an airport,' Nick said.

I stared at him a moment, like he was speaking another language. I looked around properly then, seeing other retailers getting ready to open. That's when I spotted the departures board.

'Where the fuck are we?' Jared said, looking like death and sounding like he'd had enough shit this morning already.

'It looks like we're at the wrong end of the country, my man,' Richard said as he pointed out the advertising for local hotspots plastered all over the walls. He was apparently delighted by this turn of events – smiling, slapping Jared on the back, and all round giving the impression this wasn't a complete disaster for the morning of his wedding.

'What?' I knew it wasn't helpful, but I had to get it out there for the record.

'Don't you worry yourself,' Richard said, and I ducked away from the reassuring pat on the back which was coming my way, lest it loosen another bout of chunder. 'It's early, the show doesn't start for a while yet. Let's see if we can grab a flight back.'

'But – but how did we end up here?'

'No clue…' Richard shrugged and laughed. 'Going off your current state, Arthur – Jared and Ben don't look much better, mind you – and the fact we're a good what, 600, 700 kilometres from home with no idea how we got here… I'd say we had a big night.'

'That's—'

'But, we're here now!' Richard clapped his hands – too loud, I saw Jared wince as well. 'And we've got somewhere *else* we ought to be – that is, the place where I am to marry my sweet, sweet bride. We don't have time to drive, and I think we can comfortably assume we're all still well over the limit… So, the airport is just what we need right now.'

My mind was scratching to keep up, but when it did, I couldn't argue with his reasoning.

'Let's see if there's anything going,' Richard said, heading over to the departures board.

He scanned down the flights for a moment before raising a finger in triumph. 'See, there's one, only a couple of hours away – perfect! I'll see if I can get us on that – how many tickets?' He turned to count each of us. There was Jared, eyebrows drawn together like he had a great stinking headache; Nick, not doing too badly it seemed; Jason, struggling to keep his eyes open; Ben, tinged a distinct green and wearing a blank expression; and of course myself, still quietly dying inside.

'Where are the twins?' he said.

I looked again – no lanky cousins to be seen anywhere.

'Nick,' Richard said. 'Go check the other side of the coffee shop, will you?'

Nick did as instructed and came back with one of the twins in tow. 'Found one!'

'Well, shit.' Richard reached into his pocket to check his phone.

It was dead.

The rest of us grabbed out our phones – except for Ben, who couldn't find his. They were all flat, with Nick's sporting a newly shattered screen.

'Steve,' Richard said, 'that is you, right? Yes, it is. Where's your brother?'

Still supported by Nick, he lifted his head a fraction, eyes barely open and an unreadable expression on his face. 'Kyle sneaked off – saw him – had a girl at the bar. Then they left.'

'That scoundrel!' Richard said, laughing. 'You two, full of surprises. Who knew he had it in him?'

Steve managed a grunt in response.

'Anyway, quick maths. We started the day with eight, gained Gabriel, then lost him and Kyle. That's two tickets we won't need – so that leaves us with…'

'Seven,' I said, gesturing around at the seven of us present – no maths required.

'Hah! So it is. Here we are, the seven dwarfs – we sure look as grubby as them. So who's who, then?'

It seemed fitting. Gabriel had once mentioned his measure of a hangover headache, with a scale of one to seven pickaxe-wielding dwarfs dig-dig-digging into your head. I liked it because it added an air of whimsy to an otherwise miserable state of affairs. Right now I was at a solid six.

'Oh, maybe that's it,' Richard said, snapping his fingers. 'Why we're so blacked out. Our very own Snow White – the fairest of them all – sneaked into our dwarf pub and slipped us a sprinkle of her magic flour. Might explain how we ended up so baked. Hah!'

A chorus of groans met his look of delight.

'Don't think so, mate,' said Jared, drawing his eyebrows together in laboured thought. 'Just – just too many shots is what did us in.'

'No such thing as too many shots,' Richard said. 'But never you mind, that was all last night. Right now I'm still set on giving us dwarf names…'

'What?' Jared said. I wasn't following Richard's erratic logic either. 'Just, go get the *seven* tickets and—'

'Hush now, plenty of time,' Richard said, dismissing him with a wave. 'Jared, you can be – hmm – Frowny! Steve, I dub thee Grunty. Jason is Sleepy – hah, that's a real one! Arthur, that's obvious, you can be Vommy. Nick—'

'Hungry,' he said. 'I'm hungry.'

'Yes, perfect!' Richard said. 'And Benny Boy, you're uncharacteristically quiet this morning. You can be Mime. Like Doc, you get it? More of a title than a description.'

'And what's your dwarf name to be, then?' Nick said, resigned to the charade.

'Hubby,' Jared said, like it was the most vile curse he could muster.

'Hah! Good one, Jared… Hubby!' Richard said, oblivious. 'Speaking of… would be a shame to miss my own wedding, better get those tickets – I'll see if I can get our new names on them.'

# Chapter 10
# Can't be turning up after the bride, can we?

**ARTHUR**

Richard had secured tickets, then shepherded us through the airport. I had to shade my eyes from the glare of the fluorescent lights along the way. In diverting my gaze I found myself captivated by the bag carousel as we passed the baggage claim area – the steady flow of bags snaking around, the way the conveyor belt's panels slid underneath each other as they shifted around each bend... I was mesmerised by the constant, rhythmic movement. Then it faltered for a moment, coming to a halt before lurching back into motion again. I felt my stomach lurch along with it and had to avert my eyes from the bag carousel now too.

I was still recovering from that sickening jolt of movement when we were confronted by the security checkpoint. I didn't know if I was guilty – I didn't think I was, but I also didn't *know*. Richard's comment about something slipped in our drinks – was that plausible? Would they arrest us? I tried to calm myself, to convince myself that we were all just tragic drunks, and not awash with illegal substances. Did we have anything in our pockets? I hadn't even checked, and it was too late now anyway with the eyes of aviation security on us. Or had we rubbed up against something that would set the dogs off?

This thought in my mind, I vibrated with anxiety as the sniffer dogs approached, giving us each a good snuffle – I'm sure there was much to process. Extra attention was focused on Jared's crotch, but the dog and its human soon moved on. I let out the breath I didn't realise I'd been holding in a great, rushing gust, then had to clamp my mouth shut for fear of anything else coming up.

We emptied our pockets, thankful nothing mysterious turned up, and each stepped through the metal detector without incident.

By the time we scampered out to the air-side, I was buzzing with nerves.

Now huddled around a small cafe table, strong coffees in hand, I was starting to feel like things were on the up. The coffee did nothing to calm the nerves, but it was helping a little with the hangover, and my hunger was returning while we waited for our food to arrive – a good sign.

'All right, boys,' our waitress said, sweeping up to the table, hands full of plates. 'We've got three full English breakfasts with bacon, eggs, tomatoes, bangers, baked beans, hash browns, mushrooms, and buttered toast.'

'Praise be,' Richard said.

'That's me,' Nick said.

Steve raised a finger without lifting his head or saying a word.

Our waitress slid the mounds of fried food in front of them, the hot, greasy smell almost triggering another bout of chundering. I could see Ben felt the same, looking greener than ever.

'And who ordered the pancakes?' our waitress said as she accepted more loaded plates from her colleague. 'Blueberries, strawberries, banana, with extra bacon, extra maple syrup, and extra cream?'

Jared raised a shaky hand.

'Now we have the Corn Fritters, served with streaky bacon, homemade tomato relish, and sour cream.'

Jason opened his eyes, looking confused for a moment. 'Yes, that's his.' Richard pointed with a loaded fork before jamming the hash brown into his mouth.

'Next up we have an Eggs Benedict, with our fresh spinach, homemade creamy hollandaise sauce, toasted ciabatta, and smoked salmon.'

Richard pointed his knife at Ben, mouth too full to say anything. Ben looked up in terror, then down at the plate as it was placed in front of him, his expression not changing. He didn't reach for his utensils, only stared in disgust.

'Last up we have, uh… Three slices of toasted white bread. No butter, no jam, no eggs, no nothing,' the waitress said, eyebrow raised and looking at me without attempting to hide her amusement.

'That's mine.' I was embarrassed by the order, but knew there's no way I'd hold anything else down. Everyone's food looked delicious – reminded me of Gabriel's excellence in the kitchen – but I knew I couldn't handle any of it right now.

'Enjoy your meals,' the waitress said, then she left us to it.

I donated one of my slices to Ben when after five minutes he still hadn't touched his own breakfast. He took the dry piece of toast with appreciation, nibbling off small bites, chewing and swallowing each small piece until the toast was gone. Richard and Nick were more than happy to finish off the order that Ben couldn't stomach.

## GABRIEL

'Let's take a little detour,' Claire said from the backseat, looking gorgeous in that understated way that she had – seemingly effortless.

'Drive-through cheeseburgers?' Theo said, sitting next to her and looking only a little swamped in the ill-fitting suit. 'Good idea, I haven't had breakfast and you never know what the nibbles situation will be like.'

'Sheela's in charge of the nibbles.' The thought cheered me. 'You won't go hungry.'

Theo's eyes lit up.

'Nah,' Claire said, 'let's swing by Arthur's, make sure he's functioning, put your mind at ease.'

I kept staring out the windscreen from my seat in the front, our driver on the direct route to the venue.

I sighed again – something I hadn't been able to prevent myself doing all morning – and said, 'No, we don't have time. Thanks, though.'

'Can't be turning up after the bride, can we?' I had to assume that was Theo's weak attempt to lighten the mood.

'He won't be at home, anyway,' I said. 'He'll be at the venue, straightening Richard's tie, giving him a pep talk, or whatever it is that goes on pre-ceremony.'

# ARTHUR

We should've been at the venue by now – instead we were sat on a plane. The cabin door had just been closed, and the crew were preparing for take off, so it wouldn't be long now. Despite everything, at least I wouldn't be failing that first item on the Best Man's list of responsibilities: get the groom to the wedding.

In other good news, my toast was settling nicely, the coffee was keeping me alert, and the bodyweight of water I'd drunk was dampening down some of the dustiness.

They scattered the seven of us all over the plane – the trouble with booking last minute, but we were just glad to be on board. I'd seen enough of this lot in the past 24 hours anyway – even if everything after climbing on that ridiculous party bus was a blank.

What I did know was that I was exhausted – physically and emotionally. I don't think I'd had a more active week since school camp: shooting clay birds, hitting golf balls, racing karts, shooting paintballs. This body was accustomed to spending all week sitting at a desk, with the occasional gym session tacked on.

And I was in pain. Dragging those karts around the corners near pulled my arms off. And I could feel bruises blossoming all over from the paintballs, some welts rising, too. I hated to think what other damage I'd done after hitting that memory void. Potential damage to my body, but more concerning was damage I might have done to my relationship with Gabriel – a relationship which had hardly got off the ground.

I was still disgustingly hungover, but my stomach was on the mend and my headache was down to a more manageable four out of seven pickaxe-wielding dwarfs dig-dig-digging.

That didn't stop me from missing Gabriel, mentally kicking myself for what I might have stuffed up. It was the not knowing that killed me.

And I still hadn't started writing my Best Man's speech.

## GABRIEL

'Here he is! The Best Man's best man.' Samantha swept up the aisle to kiss me on both cheeks. She looked stunning, as did the man on her arm. 'Seeing as you stole my Arthur – the man promised to me by dear Aunty Pat – I have brought along my very own handsome drink fetcher, handbag holder, and all-round dashing supporting act – you know him, you love him, it's… Cameron!'

He took a bow as Claire, Theo, and I rose from our seats. While everyone was still mixing we'd claimed a spot a few rows back on the bride's side. Claire had insisted on this side as she was good friends with Lucy, which she said trumped my second-degree connection to the groom via Arthur.

'That's quite the introduction.' I smiled at them both, giving each a hug while complimenting them on their outfits. I took the opportunity to apologise again for my substandard contributions to the quiz earlier in the week, which they graciously laughed off. It was all easy small talk with nice people I barely knew, which was fine as I couldn't really focus on them right this minute.

'And don't he look handsome, too,' Sam said, eyeing me up and down. 'Perhaps not as sparkly as I recall…'

Sam was fishing, but before I could come up with

142

anything Claire had jumped in from behind me. 'He's worried about Arthur.'

'Oh yes,' Sam said with a mischievous grin as she gave Claire and Theo a quick hug and a kiss. 'I heard the boys had a big night.'

I looked at her expectantly, and Claire and Theo were doing the same.

'What are you all – oh!' she said, laughing. 'You haven't heard?'

'Heard what?' Claire, Theo, and I said in unison.

'Yes, well, turns out the stag party did a little midnight cross-country trip.'

'What?' I said.

'Well, I'm not sure if it counts as "cross-country" if you *fly* over it.'

'What?!' Theo and Claire joined me again this time.

'Apparently, the boys got it in their heads that an impromptu getaway was in order. Saw a few snaps in the group chat I'm in with Lucy and Richard, among others. Richard posing with the airline staff at the check-in desk, Richard taking a selfie with his boarding pass, Richard licking the earlobe of one of his sleeping workmates on the plane… I think his phone died though, we didn't get any pictures after that.'

None of us said a word.

'Such a nice venue, though, isn't it?' Sam said in a jarring topic shift as she looked up and around. 'I know Lucy had her heart set on it, and now I can see why.'

When they found us still unresponsive, Sam and Cameron shuffled into our row and took a seat alongside us. 'But yes,' Sam said as she settled in, 'I do hope they make it back in time for the ceremony.'

143

We were sitting on the runway, had been for over an hour now.

The head-shaking, tutting, and tsking of the businessman to my left had increased in frequency along with a drop in subtlety as the minutes ticked by.

My frustration was mounting too, and my fellow passenger was becoming increasingly difficult to ignore. If we were moving, I might have been able to calm myself, knowing we were on our way. Or if we at least had a time frame for when we'd be underway, then I might be able to focus on what needed to be done once we landed.

I should be anxious about how this delay was gobbling up any buffer we'd had, but all I could think about was Gabriel. I was restless and nervous about how things stood between us. Worrying was pointless – I knew this – there was nothing I could do while we were at opposite ends of the country and out of communication. But something like anxiety doesn't concern itself with practicalities like that.

My seat-neighbour had taken to lifting his head to look up the aisle, then shifting around to see back in the other direction, as if anything had changed in the half-minute since he'd last looked. And when he wasn't firing off urgent text messages – each letter making a faint *tock* noise as he pressed – he was strumming his fingers on the tray table, wiping his glasses, tapping his foot, adjusting his tie, or rapping his fingernail against his tooth.

I tried my best to shut him out. But in blocking him from my mind, all I was left to think about was Gabriel, with every minute of delay another minute of agony waiting to see him. I was insufferable, neurotic, but I couldn't help myself, and the atmosphere in the cabin wasn't helping. The other passengers were getting restless now too, reflecting and amplifying my own agitation. I didn't feel the need to add my own voice to the rumbles of discontent, not when my neighbour was doing more than enough for the two of us. Instead, I quietly bristled.

The captain had come over the speakers a few times now with non-explanations that only served to fuel the discontent in the cabin. His latest announcement apologised again for the wait, expressed his hope that we'd be given the all-clear soon, asked us to remain seated unless using the bathroom, and he hoped we would enjoy the snacks and refreshments the cabin crew would be bringing around shortly.

'Unacceptable,' the businessman said in response, ostensibly to himself, but loud enough so every passenger in a three or four seat radius would hear his displeasure. And his fidgeting had ratcheted up a notch, too. It was when he took to repeatedly folding and unfolding his arms in rapid succession – each manoeuvre jostling me in my seat – that I snapped.

'Will you *sit still* and *shut up*,' I said through gritted teeth, staring him down with eyes wide. 'We all have somewhere to be. Your constant griping and fidgeting is not getting this plane in the air any bloody faster. I am tired, I have a splitting headache, I am in increasing danger of not getting the groom to his wedding on time – the Best Man's number one priority – and to top it all off, I can't be sure my boyfriend wants anything to do with me after my behaviour last night. So, *shut up* about your stinking meeting and just be still, *please*.'

He was so shocked to be spoken to in such a manner –

by a dishevelled random a couple of decades his junior, no less – that he was lost for words. Though, he recovered quickly and looked as if he was about to tell me what he thought of my outburst when the captain came over the speakers again.

'Folks, this is your captain speaking. I am pleased to announce we've been cleared for takeoff,' he said as the sound of the plane's idling engines increased in pitch and we jostled into movement. The cheer in the cabin drowned out the rest of the announcement as we taxied to the end of the runway. And as the plane sped up for takeoff, the clamour of the passengers finally settled down.

I sensed the businessman next to me taking in a deep breath and girded myself for the verbal onslaught, but all he did was breathe out again and stayed staring straight ahead – no tapping, tutting, tsking, or muttering, just silence and stillness.

I felt myself relax in response – we were on our way, for real this time.

# Chapter 11
# What do you boys call this?

## ARTHUR

There was only minimal turbulence during the flight, for which I was glad – I still hadn't regained complete confidence in my stomach. We landed after a shorter than scheduled flight – the pilot having made up time while we were in the air, yet not nearly enough to make up for the delay.

The others dashed home to wash away the sweat and the sins of yesterday before changing into their glad rags. Richard, Jared, and I headed to Richard's – where we'd hung our suits earlier in the week – to do the same, grateful to our past selves for such forward thinking.

We flew through the shower, dressed, and made ourselves as presentable as we were going to manage. We were back out again in under half an hour, conscious that the guests would be ready and waiting.

'Let them wait! What are they going to do? Start the ceremony without me?' Richard said, laughing as he pulled on his shoes at the front door. 'It's my big day, can't start the show without the man of the hour, can they? Though, better not keep my Lucy waiting too long, she might change her mind on me.'

On the way to the venue I realised we'd been in so much of a rush that I hadn't even thought to plug my phone in at the house, give it at least a little charge. It was still effectively a paperweight in my pocket. I checked the time on the car's dashboard as we pulled in – we were so late.

'Don't worry,' Richard said, waving away the frantic-looking venue staff. 'We're here, we're here.'

But all I could do was wonder if Gabriel would be here, too.

## GABRIEL

I was still staring at the spot where Richard, Jared, and Arthur were supposed to be when I noticed Sheela in the front row. How could I forget? The mother of the groom – my dear friend Sheela – turned to survey the restless crowd. She latched eyes on me and gave an anxious little wave. Nervously excited, but I could tell she was furious. Her son was making a mess of this wedding – in front of the entire family – and it hadn't even started yet.

The wedding guests had filled the seating by the appointed hour, the murmurs growing in volume, confusion, and agitation as the minutes ticked by. I hadn't been able to concentrate on the chatter between my flatmates and Lucy's nursing friends. The rising tension in the room – a lovely space apparently, not that I was able to appreciate it – only served to compound my own concern...

Where were they?

# ARTHUR

I'm sure the venue was magical.

It was the whole reason this wedding had been turned around in less than a fortnight. Which was why Richard's stag do was left till last night – on the eve of the wedding, no less. Which was why we were in such a sorry state of affairs now, the morning of the wedding. Which was why I was having trouble appreciating this supposedly fabulously romantic venue as we arrived. The day was too bright, too perfect for me to get a proper look. I was no longer in danger of bringing up my breakfast, but the litres of water and packets of painkillers I'd downed were only nibbling at the edges of my extensive headache, and I kind of needed to pee.

That's not to say I hadn't managed to resurrect a small portion of my brain's processing power, but what little capacity I'd regained was dedicated solely to wondering and worrying about Gabriel. But I won't bore you further with any more of my neuroses – suffice to say, I was in a right state.

The woman appearing in the doorway at the top of the steps pulled me back to the present. I recognised the celebrant as we made our way to the venue's side entrance. She threw up her arms in a universal gesture of vexation. 'What do you boys call this?'

'Hello, Mary. Perfect day for a wedding, isn't it?' Richard's voice was calm and pleasant, as if everything was in order. She looked like she was about to launch into a telling off, but Richard cut in. 'How do we look, then?'

She huffed, the wind taken out of her sails as she came down the stairs to fuss over us – wiping off imaginary lint, adjusting ties, and patting down stray tufts of hair.

She stepped back, looking us each up and down before turning to Richard. 'Ready?'

'Just going to pop to the gent's for a second,' Richard said.

'Me too,' Jared and I said in unison, our re-hydration efforts having finally caught up with us.

'Everyone has already been waiting for *quite some time,*' the celebrant said.

'And I'm sure they'll manage another minute or two,' Richard said as he led us inside. 'We can't be wetting ourselves at the altar, can we?'

## GABRIEL

I saw Sheela pick up her handbag, preparing herself to find out what the hell was going on, when a hush came over the crowd. That's what they say, isn't it? A bit cliché I know, but it doesn't often happen in practice, so when silence does in fact descend over a large assembled group, it's rather striking.

It had been nearly half an hour now since the advertised starting time when the harassed – but relieved – celebrant appeared in front of the gathered guests. Her arrival was met with a susurration of shushes, a rustle of fabric, and squeak of seating as everyone turned to face the front.

The celebrant settled herself on the raised platform and started her spiel – I didn't hear a word of it. Neither, it seemed, did anyone else. As one, all heads whipped to the right as the groom and his Best Men made their entrance. There was a simultaneous intake of breath across the room that quickly disintegrated into whispers of overlapping

150

chatter.

'Here they are.'

'About bloody time, let's get this show on the road.'

'Trouble in paradise.'

'Don't they look smart?'

'Having second thoughts, do you think?'

'Why are they all wearing different suits? Nothing matches.'

'I don't think I've ever seen Richard in nice clothes.'

'That bowtie on the groom though, bright yellow? Has he lost the plot?'

'What do you think kept them?'

'Last minute jitters?'

The commentary and speculation washed over me, and I didn't even notice the celebrant pause to let everyone get it out of their systems.

I heard nothing, and all I could see was Arthur, his face a picture of barely restrained anguish which clashed with the festive occasion but mirrored my own feelings leading up to this point. He was slowly and methodically scanning the guests, jolting to a halt when he found me. He brightened the moment we made eye contact, a sly little smile crossing his face – he held the look for a few seconds before returning his attention to the ceremony, visibly relaxing.

I felt myself smiling too, the worry and frustration of the past 12 hours fading in an instant.

Claire nudged my knee and gave me a reassuring smile. Any other day I might've been embarrassed by my behaviour since returning to the flat last night, but I was too relieved to care.

Turns out, Gabriel was here after all – sitting a few rows back with his flatmates and Lucy's nursing friends. The relief when I laid eyes on him, I almost collapsed with joy.

But I knew a stage faint wouldn't be a good move, especially considering the grief I'm sure we'd already caused – sauntering in well past the appointed hour and all that. I had to turn away from Gabriel – he was looking so handsome! – or I wouldn't be able to stop myself from dashing over there.

Again, not appropriate.

Now that I'd confirmed Gabriel was here, I had to focus on the job at hand. I'd got the groom to his wedding: tick. And now all I had to do was stand up on stage without fainting or running off to kiss that fine man of mine – easier said than done.

# Chapter 12
# And what are we supposed to do in the mean time?

**GABRIEL**

After the initial delay, the ceremony went flawlessly. The flower boys and girls were adorable coming up the aisle, scattering petals to beautiful music. They were followed by the bridesmaids – Lucy's sisters – in dresses of distinct styles, cuts, and colours. Nothing matched, except their bouquets, but they both looked fantastic in spite of this, or perhaps because of it? As the women got into position, I wondered how much the conflicting dresses and suits had to do with pulling the middle finger to tradition, and how much was down to the practicalities of pulling together a wedding in a week and a half. Considering the little I knew of the couple, I suspected it was a bit of both.

With the groom, groomsmen, bridesmaids, and celebrant all up the front, now it was the bride's turn.

If I thought the intake of breath at the boys' arrival was

loud, the gasp as Lucy appeared at the end of the aisle was something else – shock, wonder, delight.

Lucy was wearing a bright yellow sundress – not that I knew that's what it was at the time, but Sam confirmed for me later. I half expected her to skip up the aisle.

Instead, she walked with an occasional twist to make her dress swirl, beaming all the way as she strode to claim her man. I hadn't even met the bride yet, but I liked her style – I think we'd get along just fine. No lace or frills, no white dress of supposed innocence and chastity. Who was anybody kidding with that charade? No, she was dressed to have a good time, like she was happy to be here.

And Richard – the crassest bastard I think I've ever met with the uncanny ability to turn any situation into a farce – was bawling. A snotty, slobbery mess, wiping his eyes and nose on the back of his arm, leaving snail trails up his suit jacket – the photographer would have a real job editing that out – but it was a heartfelt, honest reaction.

He was still getting his sobbing under control when it was time for the vows. Lucy's words were light and heartwarming without being sickly sweet, and by the end I think everyone present wanted to marry her too. Richard, meanwhile, had been set blubbering all over again. He battled through his own vows, not that we could understand half of what he said through the hitches in his voice. But Lucy seemed delighted, and that's all that mattered.

The exchange of rings almost did Richard in once and for all, but he managed to hold it together as they put the rings on each others' fingers, were declared husband and wife, and walked back down the aisle.

We cheered and clapped as they passed, followed by the

rest of the bridal party. Again, I watched as Arthur hunted for me. He'd looked so happy for his friends during the ceremony, then low-key anxious again as he scanned the crowd – worried that I'd somehow vanished? – but he found me much faster now he knew where to look and his face lit up all over again.

That look felt like a stab in the chest – I found myself swallowing and blinking rapidly to hold myself together as I kept up the clapping.

*** 

The guests peeled off from the front, Sheela giving me a wink and a thumbs up as she passed down the aisle with her husband Iqbal on her arm – his tie complementing her dress perfectly, as promised.

'What's wrong with you now, Gramps?' Theo said. 'You busting for a piss?'

'What? No.' I peeled my eyes away from the row in front of us who were joining the end of the procession. 'Why?'

'You're squirming like a five-year-old on a road trip,' he said. 'A five-year-old who's just polished off a big bottle of fizzy drink.'

'Uh? No, I don't need to pee,' I said, trying to relax. 'Just ready for some fresh air. Been stuck in here for a bit longer than I thought, you know?'

'Uh huh.' Theo looked dubious, as he had every right to be. Now that I'd seen Arthur, and now the show was over, I just wanted to give him a hug. Put a pin in the whole wretched and frustrating saga that has been the past 24 hours. I knew it was illogical, but it would give me closure, and with that pave the way for the return of my composure, which was in tatters where Arthur was concerned.

Our row was next, but that only got us to the end of the long stream of people heading out. I considered making a dash down the side between the procession and the seating, but there were just too many elbows and handbags blocking the way. I'd waited this long – what difference could a minute make?

\*\*\*

We finally emerged to find guests huddled in groups in the courtyard catching up, reliving moments from the wedding we'd all just witnessed, and of course speculating about what had caused the delay.

But no Arthur.

I stepped further through the crowd, and that's when I spotted the fleet of garishly coloured muscle cars idling out on the road, the doors slamming shut one after the other. The front car – a radiant yellow to rival even Lucy's dress – revved its engine, pulling slowly away from the kerb, carrying off the married couple to wild cheers from the guests. The next car was road-cone orange and had Lucy's parents waving regally through the open windows, followed by an ecstatic-looking Sheela and her husband Iqbal in a fire-red beast with a black stripe up the middle, and last off the ranks was an acid-green monster taking away the bridesmaids and groomsmen. I didn't see Arthur's face, only the back of his head through the rear window as they turned and drove away.

'Where the fuck are they going?'

Claire tsked. 'Wedding photos, duh. Don't worry, they'll be back.'

I groaned in frustration, which felt good for a second but didn't change the situation. 'Fine! Fine… And what are we supposed to do in the mean time?' I said, quite aware how petulant I sounded but not in a mood to do anything about it.

'Mingle,' Claire said, gesturing to the crowd of Richard and Lucy's nearest and dearest.

'Eat the nibbles,' Theo said, chasing after a waiter loaded with smoked salmon crostini – where had they come from? – before changing course mid-pursuit to chase the spinach and feta filo rolls.

'Drink the bubbles,' Cameron said, swiping two flutes from a passing waiter and handing one to me.

Sam nabbed a glass each for herself and Claire. 'Come on, loverboy,' she said, elbowing me in the side. 'Let's celebrate.'

I paused a moment, realising there was nothing else for it, and raised a glass, clinking with Sam, Cameron, and Claire. Then Theo – not to be left out – got in on the action by toasting with his filo roll, smearing it against the side of our flutes before stuffing it in his mouth and rushing off to find something to wash it down with.

## ARTHUR

I'd teared up during the ceremony – I was so proud of my mate, and so happy for them both.

Despite that, I was happy for it to wrap up, meaning I could finally go and see Gabriel. Though I had to give up on that plan pretty quick as I was swept along in the procession and funnelled out to the courtyard. We paused for a few moments to get our pictures taken by the photographer before being shepherded to an old-school car painted the colour of radioactive vomit and whisked away to some stately gardens.

It felt like I was being carried along in fast-flowing floodwaters, watching helplessly as I drifted swiftly past my refuge on the shore. All very poetic, but that's how it felt now crammed in the middle seat, with Jared to my right, one of Lucy's sisters to my left, the other in the front passenger seat, and an uncle behind the wheel. These classic two-door muscle cars weren't designed for five fully grown adults, especially not ones in fancy clothes.

We traipsed all over the grounds of the estate, holding various poses with various combinations of folk. My fingers were itching to strangle the photographer when he suggested we 'do a fun one' for the nth time.

No! No 'fun ones'! Every time it's a chorus of 'Oh, no I couldn't, what am I going to do?' followed by self-deprecating chuckles. The result would invariably be 'not fun enough' or 'too fun'. These were supposed to be the nice photos of the nice people who had dressed up nicely. If you want 'fun' photos, get those later when everyone's actually having fun. Candid shots of the guests dancing and drinking and making fools of themselves, when the wheels are starting to come off – now *that* is fun.

But now, here we were with the entire bridal party, parents too, getting another picture with some prickle trees in the background.

'Arthur' – the photographer snapped his fingers at me – 'a smile, please. We can't be having frowns in front of the pink roses – a symbol of grace and joy.'

I pulled my lips back from my teeth in an attempt at a smile, determined not to draw attention to myself so we could get through this quicker.

'I think Arthur's hungry,' Jared said – his way of telling everyone that he himself was hungry. Sounded like he'd had enough of this ordeal, too.

'I'll bet Arthur is,' Richard said, 'hungry for some of Gabriel's sweet, sweet—'

'Sausage,' Jared said before breaking down laughing, Richard right there with him, doubled over and ruining the meticulously planned pose. They were losing it.

'There are some fancy little sausage rolls with the hors d'oeuvres back at the venue,' Lucy said, her stern voice lifted ever-so-slightly by her amusement.

'Oh, I don't think our boy will be satisfied with anything "little", not if he can help it,' Richard said.

'Well, Arthur will have to make do this evening – then I'm sure he'll get his fill later tonight,' Lucy said, speaking as if I wasn't right there before giving me a smile.

Richard and Jared laughed all the harder.

'Now, if you boys will stop acting up,' Lucy said, turning her school matron voice back on, 'we can be back in time before they're all eaten.'

'Yes, miss!' they said in unison.

'I mean it,' she said. 'Behave, or I'll pick one of those paintball bruises you're all sporting and drill my finger into it until you squeal.'

'Yes, miss!' they repeated, eyes wide in mock seriousness.

We managed to get through a few more poses before Richard whispered so the adults – that is, not us, obviously, the older generation – couldn't hear. 'You know what else I could do with? Something to help wash down that sausage roll.'

'Some lubrication, if you will,' Jared said.

'Can't have it going in dry.'

'Pains me to think about it.'

'I am just so thirsty.'

'Parched.'

'Will you two shut—' I attempted.

'I'm drier than a wooden tit,' Richard said.

'What?' I said, giving up any pretence at holding a pose to turn to my married friend. 'That doesn't even make sense.'

'You know it all comes back to the tits,' he said with a wink. 'Colder than a witch's tit – or a polar bear's tit, take your pick. Falling arse over tit. It's gone tits up. That's the tits—'

'All right, boys,' the photographer said, snapping his fingers from the behind the camera. 'Back over here. One more formal photo, then to finish off we'll do a fun one.'

# Chapter 13
# Who is he kidding?

## ARTHUR

I felt like royalty, sitting at the top table.

The bridal party was raised on a small stage and arranged in a line, facing out towards the peasants – more charitably referred to as 'family and friends'. The married couple – King and Queen – took centre stage, with myself and the elder of Lucy's sisters flanking the newlyweds, Jared and the younger sister beyond that. A relatively small bridal party, but you had to draw the line somewhere.

Turns out we didn't have time to mingle with the other guests once we'd returned from taking photos, and to the great disappointment of Richard and Jared the nibbles were all done, so no fun was to be had with any sausage-shaped snacks. The delayed start to the ceremony and the photographer's diligence in getting every single shot *just right* meant by the time we were dropped back at the venue we were herded straight to our thrones.

I scanned the tables arrayed before us, radiating out in

concentric rings. The tables of the first half-circle accommodated the immediate families and grandparents. One row further out included the uncles, aunties, cousins, close friends, and work colleagues the couple actually liked. I recognised most of Richard's share of these people, having been a part of his life since childhood. Kyle and Steve, the gangly twins, were there. Steve was still looking a little green after our overnight adventures, whereas Kyle was glowing, looking like an entirely new person after last night's tryst.

Nick, Jason, and Ben were at the next table along, beers in hand – hair of the dog, no doubt. They seemed to be doing OK, more experienced players than young Steve.

Then there was the outermost half-circle of tables, only partially visible in the dimmed lighting, populated by more distant family members, lesser friends, work colleagues the couple felt obligated to invite, and the 'extras'.

Lucy had admitted while we were walking back through the gardens after the photo shoot that she had serious issues with the arrangements, but having delegated the seating plan to her mother, she didn't have the time or energy to take it back. She'd picked out one table in particular. Her mother had shoved what she'd dubbed the 'extras' table into the corner – this included singles, those with unnamed plus-ones, or people the mother of the bride simply hadn't met.

And that's where I spotted Gabriel, relegated to this hospitality hinterland.

He was sitting with Samantha, who doubled as Lucy's friend from work and my neighbour's niece. She was next to another guy who looked a little familiar – perhaps a new boyfriend? I couldn't be sure, but I hoped so, that'd really get Patty off my case. Then there was another of Lucy's friends, Claire, who was also Gabriel's flatmate. She was sitting next to another guy with his back to the top table, though with the crutches leaning against his chair I presumed this was Gabriel's other flatmate, and Claire's new boyfriend, Theo. Then I think it was Ishaan and his wife Amanda who ran Richard's favourite takeaway place just down the road from mine. I must have underestimated his love for that food – enough to get an invitation to the wedding? Wow. Then there were a few others at the table, but I couldn't even begin to guess who they were.

They all looked like they were having a great time. I was glad Gabriel had some people he already knew and liked around him, considering I'd invited him to this wedding yet hadn't spent even a single moment with him. That would be my worst nightmare, being dragged along to some event then abandoned to fend for myself. Swamped by unfamiliar people I was supposed to socialise with? No, thank you.

Seeing him sitting there, I wished I could join their table, even if they were in the back corner, in partial darkness, next to the toilets. It would be a severe demotion from my current situation, but worth it, I'm sure.

## GABRIEL

Our table in Siberia appeared to be populated with the singles, new couples, and other randoms. This included Lucy's nursing friends, the brand new boyfriend of one of Richard's Best Men – that is, me – and Richard's naan dealer.

Sam took charge, deciding we needed to zip around the table introducing ourselves. A little awkwardness now saved us from the greater social discomfort of having to ask someone's name after you've already been speaking to them for an hour.

I knew most of the table already, but there were a few people on the far side who had come to the wedding together and were so boring I forgot all about them almost immediately. I felt bad, but then they didn't show any interest in interacting with anyone but themselves anyway, so I was happy to leave them to it. The only others at the table I hadn't met were Ishaan and Amanda – Richard's Indian takeaway people. Ishaan started us off by asking how I fitted into the picture.

'This guy is bonking the Best Man,' Sam said with a smirk as she finished off another glass of white.

'Jared?' Ishaan said. 'I never knew—'

'No, no, the other one: Arthur,' she said. 'Major homo, much to my aunt's disappointment.'

'Mr Extra Mild?' Ishaan said.

'Hah! What?' Sam said.

'That's what Richard calls him when he comes into the restaurant. It's how Arthur has his curries: extra mild.' Ishaan was shaking his head as if it pained him. 'Likes to pretend he can manage a "medium" curry, but who is he kidding? Poor white boy stomach – can't handle the good stuff. Though, as far as the boyfriend is concerned, probably best he sticks to bland, eh? You know, can't be giving little Arthur an upset tummy – he'll be no good to Gabriel for the rest of the night.'

With that comment he smirked suggestively, copping a slap on the shoulder from Amanda. 'Don't be so rude,' she said, whispering in his ear loud enough for all to hear. I'm glad I had her on side – I could see why Ishaan and Richard were good mates.

'Yeah, gross. We're eating!' Claire said.

'I wish,' Theo said, following the waiters with puppy dog eyes as one after another streamed past us with loaded plates smelling mouth-wateringly good, only to be set in front of guests at other tables. I could see the pattern, working its way to us last while those at the top table had almost polished off their plates already.

# Chapter 14
# Make it snappy, will you?

**ARTHUR**

By now the first course had been and gone. I'd cleared my plate without registering what I was putting in my mouth. I guess I should be thankful I wasn't worrying about keeping it down anymore. Really, I just needed us to get through the seated portion of the evening, then we'd all be free to go where we pleased – I knew where I'd be going.

'Arthur,' Richard said, getting my attention by tapping me on the back of the hand with his knife. 'What's this about your parents not being able to make it to my wedding?'

'They're on holiday, on a cruise somewhere.'

'They've gone on *holiday*? Instead of coming to *my wedding*.' Richard was outraged. 'I've known them since before I could spell my own name, and they couldn't prioritise attending the happiest day of their bonus son's life?'

'To be fair,' Jared said, leaning over, 'you only invited

166

them a week ago. They were probably in the middle of the sea already, having a grand old time.'

'I suppose,' Richard said. 'Still—'

'Would've booked the trip months ago,' Jared said, munching on a miniature bun – we had a whole basket of them just for the three of us. 'Cost a bomb too, I imagine – a week or two on those big boats isn't cheap.'

'True… And probably for the best,' Richard said. 'You know how Denise gets me all fired up.'

'Mate!' I said, an urgent whisper. 'You're sitting right next to your wife of two or three hours. And, I feel like I'm obligated to remind you, though it's pointless, this is my *mother* you're talking about. My mother, who is twice your age and still very much with my father.'

'Yes, yes,' Richard said, waving me away, still wielding that knife. 'You have mentioned once or twice. And, as I say, it's for the best. It could've got awkward, considering the simmering sexual tension Denise and I share—'

'The tension is very much one-sided.'

'—she'll have to accept I'm off limits now… Though, maybe when Lucy starts getting bored with me she'll be open to the idea of inviting Denise to join us, you know, spice things up with a—'

'Anyway,' Jared said, cutting Richard off with his mouth still full, halfway through another diminutive loaf of bread. 'What do your parents think of Gabriel?'

'Yes, can my dear Denise feel the heat of that sexual tension – or should I say, frustration – pulsing between you two lustbirds?' Richard said, gesturing between me and the distant Gabriel.

'What?'

'I can feel it radiating off you,' Richard said. 'And don't

167

think I haven't caught you glancing over at that shady corner every four or five seconds.'

'Yeah, watch it or you'll put your neck out,' Jared said, washing down his bun with a gulp of Champagne.

'They – uh – they haven't met him yet,' I said.

'What?' Jared said. 'Why not?'

'What's the hold-up?' Richard added. 'He's hot, and a gentleman too, so you know he'll play well to the parental crowd.'

'I haven't told them I'm gay yet, either,' I said.

Jared and Richard sat there in silence, jaws hanging open, then Jared clipped me on the ear.

'Ow! What the—'

'Get a bloody move on, mate,' Jared said.

'Gabey-baby's not going to hang around as your dirty little secret for long. You need to show him you mean business.' Richard shook his head. 'I'm embarrassed for you.'

'You know we'll back you up,' Jared said, emphasising his point with another bun. 'Don't you?'

'Yeah, I—'

'And Gabriel's worth it,' Jared said.

'So worth it,' Richard said, crowding me from the other side.

'I mean, he's banging.'

'Decent, too.'

'A gift from above.'

'Living up to his name, isn't he?'

'You two should get hitched,' Jared said.

'Ah, bit premature, don't you—'

'Wash your mouth out,' Richard said, slamming the table. 'There will be no talk of anything premature – not on *my* wedding night. And don't worry, I'll sort out your stag do – least I can do.'

'Oh no, not a chance.'

'Least I can do.'

'I think we're getting ahead—'

'Here we are,' our waiter said, arriving with our main courses.

I was grateful for the interruption. I already knew I had to tell my parents and felt justified maintaining the position that I hadn't had the time. It was only two weeks ago that I told the boys – the first I'd ever mentioned it to another soul. Since then I'd been busy with work, spending time with Gabriel, days out with my friends – young and old – and my parents hadn't even been in the country for half that time. To be fair to me, I've had a bit going on.

Our waiter placed three plates down in front of the male half of the table, while a second did the same at the other end.

I was always simultaneously nervous and impressed watching waiters carrying hot, loaded dinner plates, one in each hand and a third balanced on their forearm. This while dodging distracted adults and wild children on their journey to the table, acknowledging someone at another table who simply must have their water topped up this instant, and then remembering who ordered what meal when they finally delivered the food.

The whole thing was a real art that I'd never mastered during my brief stint at a cafe during university. Not only does dropping a plate result in broken crockery, you make a noise, cause a scene, and spray untouched food all over the floor. This does not endear you to the chef who's had their work wasted, or the cafe owner who has just had any profit from that table tipped in the bin. Fingers crossed the loss of one plate doesn't cause you to overcompensate and lose the second and third plate to the tiles as well. Needless to say, after my second incident I was happy to limit myself to one plate per hand on the recommendation of the manager.

But now, as the guest, I could appreciate the food without stressing about getting it to the table in one piece. It looked and smelt delicious, quite literally mouth-watering. I found myself wanting to know what Gabriel thought – he was the real foodie, and knew how to cook, too. I only knew how to eat. And even though I didn't understand the ins and outs, I could still appreciate a tasty, well-crafted meal.

I was forgetting myself – ever since I'd worked in hospitality, I've had mad respect for waitstaff who can pull this all off. As the one being served, the least I could do was acknowledge them with brief eye contact and a 'thank you.'

I looked up from the food. Our waiter was lean and tall, with familiar curly brown hair, fair skin and a dusting of freckles across his nose.

'Hot off the press for my three favourite boys,' he said with a smile. 'And straight to the *top* table.' He gave me a wink at that.

'Noah!' Richard said, jumping up for a hug. 'Mate, what are you doing here?'

I'd had trouble placing him out of context to begin with, but of course.

'I'm at the cafe in the mornings, working till the early afternoon, and sometimes I've got weddings here on the weekends. Got to keep hustling till I snag myself a sugar daddy, don't I?'

'Too right, my man.'

'But today's not about me... I do believe congratulations

are in order,' Noah said. 'Well done, she's gorgeous.'

'Thank you. She is, isn't she?' Richard said with real sincerity, turning to look at his wife briefly.

'Oh, it's too much!' Noah said, before whipping his head to me. 'And what about you, my King Arthur at the high table?'

Before I could answer, he turned to Jared and Richard. 'I'm sorry to say, but your boy here has been cheating on you,' he said with mock gravity. 'Brought another man to my cafe the other week.'

'He did not,' Jared said, his face already stuffed with food.

'Vile beast!' Richard said, slamming down the cutlery he'd just picked up.

'Oh no, this was no monster,' Noah said. 'An angel in fact, reputed to have the most heavenly touch.'

'Mm, yes, we've heard about this touch,' Richard said. 'Looked after our poor invalid and raised him back up to good health.'

'We approve of Gabriel,' Jared said. 'He's over there in the corner.'

'Is he now?' Noah gave me a sly smile. 'I think I'll have to assign myself to that table – oh, looks like things are happening,' he said, looking off to the side. 'I'd best be off. You boys behave yourselves tonight.'

Richard smiled and waggled his eyebrows as Noah stepped away.

Richard's uncle – one of many – was up again with the microphone, clearing his throat. Sheela had recruited him for the role of master of ceremonies. 'He's a shocking drunk,' Richard had said earlier. 'He's been given the responsibility – and the hard word from Mum. He knows it's an important job – I wouldn't inflict it on my worst enemy – so he'll keep it together, stone-cold sober until his duties are done, which won't be till near the end of the night. Hah! Mum has stitched him up right proper.'

'And now we'll be hearing a few words from Richard's Best Men: Jared and Arthur. Over to you, boys,' the uncle said. Then, with his mouth well away from the microphone, he said to us, 'Make it snappy, will you? I'm dying of thirst up here.'

I was still smirking at the thought of Richard's poor uncle being put to work while everyone else was enjoying themselves when I registered why he'd said my name: it was time for the Best Men's speech.


## GABRIEL

Despite the MC's best efforts – introducing each speaker with an unsubtle reference to how long their address ought to be – the speeches went on. I endeavoured to maintain interest in the others, but I only had ears for Arthur's.

I had one hand clasped in the other, resting on the table to prevent them shaking as Arthur readied himself to speak. He looked as if he was about to fall apart. It was all I could do to stay seated and stop myself rushing up to give him a big hug.

Claire, sitting to my right, gave me a smile and a nudge. As if I wasn't *well* aware that it was almost Arthur's turn. And Sam, on my left, stayed looking forwards but rested her hand lightly on my forearm. It was strangely reassuring, especially when I had no reason to be anxious. I wasn't the one addressing a room full of people with great and contradictory expectations. The speech had to be light and amusing yet meaningful and heartwarming, extensive and thorough yet brief and to the point – in a word: impossible.

# Chapter 15
# Who was he talking about up there?

**ARTHUR**

Thankfully, Jared grabbed the microphone first, launching into a string of tasteless anecdotes, the vast majority of which I had either been involved in, or witness to. Though I was only listening with half an ear, frantically trying to figure out what I was going to say. This speech was something I had definitely procrastinated on, thinking inspiration would come tomorrow, or maybe the next day. Worse than that, I'd put off even *thinking* about it because that just stressed me out.

And now here we were. A minute or two away from Jared passing over the microphone, everyone's attention on me – Gabriel's included – and I had to spit out something heartfelt yet humorous, pithy yet witty.

With Jared playing for laughs and cringes, I knew I had to lean into genuine and thoughtful. I'd barely formed this thought when I heard my name, followed by silence and a microphone in my face.

I stared at it a moment, before raising my hand to take it and stand up. All of this I was doing slowly – the longer it took to get into position, the longer it would be before I had to say *something*, let alone anything meaningful. Unfortunately, the entire time I was dragging out the process, all I was thinking about was how I was dragging out the process, not putting my mind to coming up with my impromptu speech.

'Uh – so, yeah. I'm Arthur,' I said, clearing my throat and taking a gulp of my Champagne.

Short and sweet, that's all we need – in and out.

'So… Richard, Jared, and I have been friends since forever' – no, too far back, fast-forward – 'as Jared probably already mentioned, but I wasn't really listening.'

I was rambling, explaining myself and prolonging the pain because of it. But my last half-mumbled comment garnered a few chuckles around the room. Perhaps I should shoot for honesty…

'If I'm being truthful, I'm not accustomed to situations like this – Richard and Jared are the more public-facing members of our little threesome.' More chuckles and a few chokes of surprise. 'You know what I mean… Us three have done everything together since we were boys – well, near enough.'

I had a sip of my wine and took a breath while my audience composed themselves.

'I'm terribly disorganised, but also highly strung, which is not a winning combination, let me tell you. I'd forgotten I was giving a speech tonight until Jared got up to talk – I'll admit it's been a jittery few minutes. And that, after an already nerve-racking day. Did Jared mention we woke up at the wrong end of the country? This morning? Mm. A story for another day perhaps, once we've all recovered.'

I shook my head briefly and flexed my sweaty fingers around the slippery microphone.

'What I'm *trying* to say is that we've always been there for each other – Richard, Jared, and me. In his way, Richard makes me a better person for being his friend, even if he does it in unconventional ways. Which tend to put me on the verge of full-scale meltdowns, but that's by the by. Even though Lucy is ten times better than us, she chose Richard – she supports him, pushes him, and tells him to pull his head in when he needs to. She makes him a better, happier person. I only hope that she's getting something out of this arrangement, too.'

Lucy smiled, and Richard gave a cocksure nod, earning hoots of approval from the crowd.

'She must be,' I said, 'considering she's the one who put a ring on it.'

That got a round of cheers from the room, and it was a few moments before I could speak again.

'Then she sealed the deal today at this wonderful wedding, less than two weeks after popping the question. It's a testament to how much these two are loved by the people in their lives that everyone dropped what they were doing to be here at such short notice.'

I had to pause again while the room calmed down.

'What Richard and Lucy have shown me is that you shouldn't muck around. When you know, you know, and that's when you need to do something about it.'

I turned to Richard and Lucy, raised my glass, and smiled. 'My dear friends, I wish you all the happiness in the world.'

Everyone cheered and glasses clinked around the room. I collapsed in my chair, relieved to have got through without making a complete tit of myself.

Richard was on me the moment I sat back down, giving me a big kiss and a hug. 'Thanks, mate,' he said. 'That meant a lot.' And he was sincere – no bawdy jokes, just genuine feeling.

I took the gratitude but felt guilty doing so, unsure who that speech had been directed at near the end – Richard and Lucy, or myself.

## GABRIEL

The hors d'oeuvres earlier had been delicious, and I would be sure to congratulate my dear friend Sheela on her culinary triumph. My hand had itched to snatch one from every plate that wandered past, but instead I'd restrained myself, savouring each bite, taking my time with small breaks between morsels. I was being sensible, not wanting to get bloated and spoil my dinner – mustn't peak too early with the food. Also, I didn't want to stuff my face and come across as some greedy gannet.

That was a mistake.

We were all starving now – the nibbles and the first course a long-faded memory of a past life.

Even reflecting on Arthur's speech wasn't enough to distract me for long. Claire had caught it too, so I knew I wasn't making it up. 'Who was he talking about up there?' she'd said to me after Arthur had sat back down. 'Near the end, I mean.' I admitted I'd been wondering the same thing myself. She'd smiled at that, taking a sip of her wine before turning away to leave me to my thoughts.

However, my attention was soon drawn back to my hunger by my rumbling stomach. It appeared the other guests at my table felt the same as we were making admirable progress on the baskets of small bread loaves, alternating bites with gulps of wine. We kept this up, basket after basket, until the waiters delivering dinner had nowhere else to go.

'We're next,' Theo said, a wild look in eyes. 'We're next.'

'Oh, we're truly sorry, but we've run out of the main course,' Sam said in an apologetic and deferential tone. 'What we can certainly offer is some more complementary bread baskets – a selection of our freshly baked ciabatta and dinner rolls, paired with artisanal butters and oils. That ought to tide you over until the cake is cut.'

'They wouldn't *dare*,' Ishaan said, dropping his napkin on the table and pushing back his chair. 'I'm going to have a word.'

'Sit down,' Amanda said, pulling him back into his seat. 'I'm sure it'll be fine.'

And so it was. As soon as she'd said it, five waiters streamed from the kitchen, a plate in each hand, sweeping around the table until they encircled us, evenly spaced between guests, then simultaneously set down a plate to each side. I almost wanted to clap – firstly for the theatre, but also for finally receiving our meals.

I looked up to thank my waiter – it's only good manners.

'Hello Gabriel,' he said with a smile.

I started at the familiar face. 'Oh, hi! Didn't – uh – didn't expect to see you here.'

'What can I say... I get around.' He shrugged and laughed. 'And on that note, I have to go – love you and leave you, as they say – much to do behind the scenes! Was nice to see you again, Gabriel.'

'You too, Noah,' I said, and realised I'd meant it. My ill-conceived notion that big cities allowed you some small measure of freedom and anonymity had taken yet another hit, and I feared it might be time to abandon the notion altogether. But perhaps that wasn't so bad after all, not when—

Noah ducked back, interrupting my thoughts. And speaking so only I could hear, he said, 'I forgot to say, your Arthur is looking rather a lot like his legendary namesake up there tonight, isn't he?'

I smiled and laughed even as I felt my cheeks heating up. 'He is.'

'Well done, Gabriel,' he said with a pat on my shoulder. 'He's a keeper.'

I didn't trust myself to speak, nodding once instead.

Noah smiled in return and rushed off again to the kitchens.

'You're a shameless flirt, Gabriel,' Sam said, smirking as she picked up her cutlery. 'And with your man sat just over there – outrageous!'

'It's him we were talking about, actually,' I said.

'Is that so? Another rival for Arthur's affections, is he? That old girl didn't even know about this one…' Sam shook her head. 'Oh, speaking of, did I tell you about Nora and Desmond? Those oldies at the driving range making eyes at each other?'

'What about them?'

'Well, on the drive back to the retirement village, they took the back seat together.'

'They did not.'

'They did,' Sam said, smirking with delight. 'Got to know each other a bit better, didn't they?'

'Kids these days.' I tutted and picked up my water glass.

'And you'll never guess what happened…'

'What's that?' I said as I took a sip.

'Aunty Pat caught them.'

I snorted, the water I'd only half-swallowed coming back up and shooting out my nose.

'Heard banging and crashing at the back of the coach, thought something was wrong, didn't she? Heart attack or something,' Sam said, laughing as I mopped up the water. 'So she went to investigate.'

Eyes wide, I shook my head in wonder as I regained my composure.

'Aunty Pat copped a fair eyeful, based on all her coughing and spluttering, anyway,' Sam said, still chuckling. 'She was too shocked to even protest! Just scurried back to her seat. Can you imagine?'

I was laughing now, too. 'Those old horndogs.'

'Heart rates were certainly up. No heart attack, though,' Sam said. 'And then I overheard—'

'I think I get the picture,' I said, cutting her off before she regaled me with any further details.

'No, no. I expect they were a little embarrassed after that interruption, so they settled down,' Sam said, lips pursed in delight. 'But shortly after I overheard an invitation for a nightcap when they got home.'

'And?'

'And it was accepted, I am pleased to report.'

'Good on them.' I nodded in approval.

'To love,' Sam said, raising her wine for a toast, 'whenever, whoever, and however it strikes.'

We clinked glasses.

'To love,' I said, taking a sip. And as I placed my glass back down I found myself unable to avoid glancing towards the top table.

'Eat your dinner,' Sam said, tapping my plate with her fork, 'before it gets cold.'

I pulled my eyes back to our own table to see Sam already munching away. Looking down at my plate, I gave myself a mental shake – how could I have forgotten about *this*? I was ready to devote my full attention to the food.

First impressions: the plating was masterful. So beautiful I almost didn't want to cut into it – but who was I kidding? My mouth was producing so much saliva so fast it almost hurt.

The pork belly looked so tender, so juicy, with an over-sized shard of crackling resting on top.

'Like a big delicious race-day hat for Miss Piggy,' Sam said.

'Wear the carcass of your kin, but make it fashion,' Cameron said, snapping off a corner with his teeth. 'I call it "cannibal chic."'

'So morbid!' Sam scoffed.

The crackling was puffy and crisp, crunching as I bit into its salty deliciousness. I set the rest of Miss Piggy's hat aside, saving it for later while I sampled the pork belly itself, the kumara puree, the sesame-dressed slaw, and the broccolini bathed in hot butter. Finally, I broke open the deep fried ball of rice, mozzarella, and spices, all coated in breadcrumbs – the hot cheese stretching as I put a segment of the arancini in my mouth. I circled my plate, revisiting each of the delicious flavours I'd rationed for myself. This was no mass-produced wedding fare – I recognised the hand of my friend, the mother of the groom, Sheela in the creation of this meal. After numerous laps of small, restrained mouthfuls, I crunched down on the final broken shard of pork crackling.

My plate was spotless, and I was satisfied. I sat back and relaxed into my chair – culinary bliss.

'Enjoy that, did you?' Claire said, smirking.

'What?' I said, my taste buds still floating down from on high.

'Exactly. I've been trying to get your attention for the past minute or so,' Claire said. 'Probably couldn't hear us over all your groaning and sighing and mmm-ing.'

'Why? What's happening?' I said, looking around the table to see everyone already facing the front of the room, a look of polite anticipation on their faces.

'It's time to cut the cake,' she said.

'I've only just finished my—'

Claire shushed me, so I shut up, took a gulp of wine and turned to watch the show – intermission over.

# Chapter 16
# What do you call that, darl?

## ARTHUR

My attention had wandered over to Gabriel again – even though I could barely see him in the shadows, I knew he was there. I was busy thinking about what I might do with Gabriel in a dimly lit corner when a shining white, three-tiered behemoth was carefully set down in front of the married couple, the scale and brightness of it enough to catch my eye and drag my mind up from the sewer.

Richard turned to his bride and said in his most theatrical voice, 'What do you call that, darl?'

'Wedding cake.' Lucy had no time for Richard's nonsense when their guests were all looking their way.

'Beautiful!' Richard said, looking around to me and Jared, impressed. 'And what's that stuff on top?'

'Fondant.' Lucy sighed as she picked up the massive knife. 'Now, are you going to help me cut this cake or not?'

'Of course, of course,' Richard said, hands up in surrender, eliciting laughter from all around the room.

Richard and Lucy joined their hands on the knife's handle and the room quietened. The couple made the first cut with the hovering photographer snapping a flurry of shots as everyone cheered.

Then, with the show now over, everyone swiftly returned to their drinking and chatting. Lucy took charge, carving pieces for the six of us at the top table, before the staff took it away to cut up for the guests.

Richard handed me and Jared our pieces, then waited for us to take a bite. 'How is it, boys?' Richard said.

'Good,' I said, and Jared nodded his agreement.

'That's good, because we'll be trotting out the leftovers for dessert night after night till it's all gone,' Richard said.

Jared and I were less enthusiastic in our response to that.

'Did I tell you Mum and Dad still have a whole tier of their wedding cake at the bottom of the freezer in the garage,' Richard said.

'What? Why?'

'No idea. I mean, who would want to save that?' Richard said. 'I understand what it represents, the significance, and it'll look fantastic in the photos. But the cake itself? Not great. Inflict as much of it as you can on your wedding guests, I say, then mop up what's left as soon as. Get rid of the nasty thing.' Richard stopped himself, turning slightly to see Lucy looking our way. 'Except *our* wedding cake, of course. I was talking about other people's wedding cakes. *Ours* is lovely.'

Richard jammed another loaded forkful into his mouth as the long-suffering Lucy rolled her eyes and tucked into her own piece.

# GABRIEL

The moment the final bite of wedding cake was in my mouth, my plate was snatched away. Our table had the dubious distinction of enduring the long tease waiting to be served while all around everyone was eating or had even finished already, only to be bookended by being given the hurry-up to finish our course as proceedings were moving on.

'Is that the food all done?' Theo said.

'Lucy mentioned dessert would come out later and be a free-for-all style thing,' Sam said. 'Plenty left on the agenda yet, though: more drinks and dancing and relatives making dicks of themselves.'

'Ah, weddings,' Claire said, raising a toast.

'Are they going to let us up from this table beside the toilets now, then?' Ishaan said.

'Cheers to that,' I said, taking a gulp from my drink. I was also privately celebrating that I might finally get to see Arthur from less than 20 metres away. We hadn't been in any form of contact – other than glances across the room – since I'd rushed off last night. I was itching with impatience now the time was upon us.

I downed the rest of my drink and topped it up again as the MC tapped the microphone and cleared his throat. 'Family and friends, please be upstanding and make your way over for the couple's first dance.'

# Chapter 17

# That's not how this works, is it?

### ARTHUR

What sounded like a string orchestra blasted from the speakers as guests made their way from the tables to the edge of the brightly lit dance floor.

I felt the tickle of recognition, but it wasn't until the vocals kicked in that I recognised the song as Aerosmith's *I Don't Want to Miss a Thing.* Accompanied by Steven Tyler's crooning, Lucy led Richard out to the centre of the dance floor. With arms around each other, they rocked side to side, unable to take their eyes off each other. The classic rock power ballad washed over me. At any other time, this music might have seemed corny, but here and now as I watched my friends in their own little world featuring only each other, overwhelmed with joy, it tugged at my heartstrings and my tear ducts alike.

The couple had the dance floor to themselves for a

minute, their family and friends watching on from the sidelines, before Lucy's bridesmaids took to the floor.

I stepped after them – it being traditional for the groomsmen and bridesmaids to pair off after the couple – but Jared shot out a hand to rest on my arm. We watched the bridesmaids lead their boyfriends out onto the floor instead.

That's not how this works, is it?

Jared smiled and shrugged – looked like we wouldn't be dancing with the sisters after all. Then he nodded in the direction I'd been glancing all night before stepping out to take the hand of a delighted Sheela, mother of the groom, for a dance.

I found myself alone.

Alone and exposed on the edge of the dance floor.

Richard and Lucy's family and friends were all gathered, eyes following the dancing couples, and waiting for me to join them. Only then would the rest of the guests make their way onto the dance floor.

I scanned the crowd until I spotted Gabriel.

He was already staring right back at me.

This gorgeous man, all mine. That is, if I didn't screw this up, or hadn't screwed it up already. To think I'd dithered coming out, finding the right time. There was no bloody right time. But there was the right guy...

Gabriel was that guy.

He was too important to lose, and it felt like this was the moment the past few weeks had been building up to. Injuring my back and getting to know Gabriel when I thought he was just a diligent employee with misplaced guilt. My birthday drinks, the well-meaning harassment from my friends at the Sunset Villas and from my best mates Richard and Jared...

It was a lot, and over such a short space of time. But I knew I couldn't muck around with this, with Gabriel – it was now or never.

## GABRIEL

I took one step forwards, eyes still locked on Arthur's – an invitation, a suggestion, a challenge.

Arthur stared right back for a moment longer before stepping into the light, striding across the open dance floor and embracing me in a vicelike hug, pinning my arms to my sides and holding me close.

It was only for a second, then he held me at arm's length, smiled with pride in his eyes, and pulled me back onto the floor where the other couples were stepping and swaying to the soaring music.

Standing in the middle of the dance floor, he looked me right in the eyes, more handsome than ever, and laced his fingers in mine. He lifted my other hand onto his shoulder, placing his own around my waist—

Hang on – this bastard was trying to lead.

I lifted his hand up to *my* shoulder before replacing mine around *his* waist. But before we could get moving, he'd switched us back again, a sly grin on his face.

Arthur lifted his mouth to my ear and said so I could hear over the music, 'I'm taking charge.'

He pulled away and I'm not sure what he saw on my face, but he leaned in again. 'At least for the next few minutes,' he said, his breath hot on my ear for a second before pulling back.

I'd come to this city to escape my small town, find my

own way without the weight of expectations. To be independent, to be free. Then this guy runs into me – quite literally – and forces me to reassess what I'm about, even though he's in the middle of sorting himself out too.

This guy, with the biggest heart, surrounded by people who loved him – young and old. They were drawn to him, and I found myself being pulled in as well.

There's only so self-reliant you can be before what you really become is lonely. And there was no chance of that with Arthur bringing to the table his very own claustrophobia-inducing cast of characters.

Arthur made me realise I wanted to share – that I wanted to be a part of something. And who knew, letting him take charge on occasion… I might even enjoy it.

This had all rushed through my mind as he pulled our bodies in close. We pressed against each other and I knew I wouldn't have it any other way. He clamped his arm firmly across my lower back, smiled and took the first step.

Happy to be here with him, I smiled right back and followed his lead.

I wanted to see where this would take us.

# Thank you for reading

I hope you enjoyed the story. If you did, please tell your friends – personal recommendations are the best! Also please consider leaving reviews on Amazon and Goodreads. This is important in making my work more visible to other readers – each review gives the books a little boost in the charts, meaning others are more likely to stumble across them.

For my latest updates and a free short story you can join the mailing list on my website: www.gbralph.com. You can also find my other stories there, and links to my social media if you'd like to drop me a message – I'd love to hear from you!

# Acknowledgements

Following our return to New Zealand in the second half of 2020, we spent two weeks in a managed isolation hotel, as all returning Kiwis have been required to do during the Covid-19 pandemic.

We are so grateful for the hard work and commitment of fellow Kiwis and the government in keeping New Zealand safe during this awful time. We now find ourselves in the privileged position of enjoying relatively normal everyday life, something we do not take for granted.

It wasn't easy getting back, though. With the Covid-19 situation in constant flux, our flights were delayed or cancelled multiple times. And when we did manage to get on our way, the journey back took *44 hours*.

For anyone wondering how you could possibly spend that long travelling, our journey involved getting the DLR and tube to Heathrow with plenty of time to spare, only to kick around the airport for a few hours before getting on a 12 hour flight to Hong Kong. It's a long time, but to be fair, the flight wasn't so bad as we had a row to ourselves – each! – so could spread out a bit. Then, because of issues with cancellations, we had an 11 hour stopover in the very empty, mostly shuttered Hong Kong airport. Our next piece of good fortune was a flight attendant friend contacting the cabin crew of our next flight, who gave us a very warm welcome on the second major leg of our journey. That was something special, and quite heartwarming after so much stress and uncertainty leading up to that point. Next up: an 11 hour flight to Auckland, but again with the luxury of a row each. Upon landing, we were told we'd all be flown on a chartered domestic flight to our managed isolation hotel *somewhere else*. At this stage, what's another few hours? So, more time waiting at the airport, another flight, and finally a shuttle to the hotel.

It may have been 44 hours of heightened anxiety, mask wearing, constant hand sanitising, and catching naps whenever we could, but I think our experience was relatively cushy.

Still, by the time we arrived at the managed isolation hotel, I was zonked.

So, when the hotel staff member asked if we needed a twin or double room, my thoughts went something like this: 'Two or two? What's wrong with this guy? There are two of us standing here, obviously. So we need a room for two people.' I'm glad I didn't say any of this out loud, instead opting for the more articulate, 'Sorry, what?'

I hadn't realised our friendly and patient shift manager was asking if we were a couple requiring one bed (i.e. a double room), or just friends requiring two beds (i.e. a twin room). My partner, who still had some of his wits about him, stepped in to confirm that we needed a double room. Our new friend smiled and said, 'I'll get you the suite.'

And so he did. Our room was a spacious suite on an upper floor, with views out two sides across the city and beyond. It was a very comfortable space to spend two weeks.

Getting knocks on the door – a break in the monotony! – was the other highlight of our stay. This either meant our meals had been dropped off, or a nurse was here to take our temperature or swab the back of an eyeball via a nostril.

What I'm trying to say is we had a lot of time and very few distractions. I used some of this time to tidy up the admin and hit 'publish' on *Slip and Slide*.

So, a massive thank you to all the healthcare, hospitality, cleaning, catering, government, and army staff involved in running the managed isolation and quarantine facilities – you're all champions.

Following our release from managed isolation, we felt lucky to catch up with family and friends from home – in person! Over this time I was already laying the groundwork for Arthur and Gabriel's next instalment, so when the first wave of get-togethers was over I was ready to dive straight into the first draft of what would become *Over and Out*. It was great spending time following the characters' escapades while my partner and I settled back into New Zealand life.

Now, while we're in the neighbourhood…

It goes against my sense of self-respect as a New Zealander to praise anything Australian, but *The Castle* deserves all the adoration it gets. Endlessly quotable, the 1997 comedy-drama film is a classic – as relevant today as it ever was. The sense of justice, taking joy in the little things, the importance of family, the humour, rooting for the underdog, and sticking it to the big guy. If you've seen the film as many times as I have, you may have noticed a few allusions made or lines paraphrased in this book. And if you haven't seen *The Castle*, you're in for a treat.

Thank you to my partner, Te Peeti, for assuring me this book, unlike the year 2020, wasn't a steaming pile of rubbish. And, as has become his habit, for finding another page one typo. This time the culprit was 'impeachable' when I clearly meant 'unimpeachable' – an important distinction. As teachers are so quick to point out, I was just making sure he was paying attention. And by now, I think he'd feel shafted if I didn't leave a little Easter Egg for him to find in the form of a typo.

Thank you again to Alex and Cam, for all your valuable comments and suggestions. Reminding me to rescue abandoned story threads, pointing the finger at clunky or ambiguous sentences, and helping with that final polish that made this book the best it could be.

And finally I want to thank *you,* dear reader, for following Arthur and Gabriel's antics. We may revisit them in future – who knows? – but for now at least, this is where we leave them. I hope you've had as much fun with these guys as I have, and I'll see you again soon.

Printed in Great Britain
by Amazon